T0146748

Simon & Schuster

New York London Toronto

Sydney Tokyo Singapore

Too Easy

a novel

Bruce Deitrick Price

SIMON & SCHUSTER
Rockefeller Center
1230 Avenue of the Americas
New York, New York 10020

This book is a work of fiction. Names, characters, places, and incidents are either products of the author's imagination or are used fictitiously. Any resemblance to actual events or locales or persons, living or dead, is entirely coincidental.

Designed by Karolina Harris
Manufactured in the United States of America

10 9 8 7 6 5 4 3 2 1

Library of Congress Cataloging-in-Publication Data
Price, Bruce D., date.
Too easy : a novel / Bruce Deitrick Price.
p. cm.
1. Man-woman relationships—New York (N.Y.)—Fiction.
2. Newspaper editors—New York (N.Y.)—Fiction.
3. Marriage—New York (N.Y.)—Fiction. 4. Murder—
New York (N.Y.)—Fiction. I. Title.
PS3566.R44T66 1994
813'.54—dc20 94-5735
CIP

ISBN: 978-1-5011-4091-4

AFFECTIONATELY DEDICATED TO
MY BROTHERS

BEAU AND WAYNE

(Guys who don't read novels . . .
but now they'll have to read this one.)

When we want to read
of the deeds that are
done for love,
whither do we turn?
To the murder column.

—George Bernard Shaw

Part

I

Chapter 1

Robert walks toward the water fountain, frowning, wondering how he's going to handle this thing. Two of his best reporters want the bank story. The one who wants it most is least suited for it. They're yelling at each other in his office.

Why can't people be reasonable? But then, he thinks, they wouldn't be working for a newspaper, would they?

He's not wearing his jacket, the shirt sleeves are rolled up. He's a tall man, just turned thirty-six, maybe an athlete once but a little soft around the middle now. The brown hair is long. He walks with a big man's slow confidence, smiling absently to himself. Damned reporters, he thinks, if they're not a little crazy they're no good, isn't that the truth?

Robert snaps out a cup, fills it from the water fountain. So, what's it going to be, which maniac gets the story, and what does the loser get?

Robert drains the cup, puts it down, sees a woman he

doesn't know. She smiles as though he does. Standing only a few feet in front of him. He makes an expression that says, Yes?

"Oh," she says, "I'm Kathy Becker. In marketing." She tilts her head, still smiling. "You must be Robert Saunders . . . the distinguished managing editor."

"You want—" he gives her a quizzical smile—"what?"

She puts out her hand. "People always *want* something. Must be rough."

He shakes her hand. Warm, strong. He sees the dark hair, not too long, the good-looking face, perhaps midwestern. He glances down for a second. She's dressed in a subdued way, a little formal for the office, maybe for something after work. Still, it's a tailored outfit and he gets a sense of her as trim, in good shape. Actually, great shape.

"Sorry," he says. "Well, as a matter of fact, they usually do. That's my job, basically. Telling people what they can't have." He almost laughs, thinking that's fairly witty.

"Well, you're home free," she says. "I don't want anything." She shrugs her shoulders. "I've been working here a month or so. Bound to run into you eventually. Uh, your picture's in the annual report."

"Oh, yeah. . . . Right."

"Of course, in person, you're . . . "

His eyebrows go up. *Yes?*

She laughs. "Larger."

Maybe that's funny, he's not sure. It's cute. Anyway, she's cute. "Right," he says.

She's still looking at him the same way, smiling, tilting her head to the side. In a way he thinks of as flirtatious or close to it. He turns a little away from her, glancing back toward the large open office. Twenty people working at desks. Maybe, he thinks, she's trying to make somebody jealous. No, nobody's watching them. She can't be flirting with me, he thinks. She must have seen the thick gold ring on his left hand.

He leans to fill the cup again. Something to do. "Marketing? What's that mean?"

"Fancy word for advertising. We make people buy the paper. Or maybe an advertiser needs a little help, we can do that."

"Oh, creative," he says, as though it's a slightly risqué word. Sipping the water more slowly this time.

"On a good day," Kathy says brightly. "Oh, I heard some people talking about you."

"Good God—gossip!"

"No, quite harmless. Seems you went white-water rafting."

"Oh, well, that was in the fall. Yeah, made it down the Delaware in one piece."

"Sounds very adventurous." Again the warm smile. "Maybe dangerous."

"Only for the rocks," he says.

"Come again."

He waves vaguely. "We hit them a lot."

"Oh. No, really, it sounds very exciting. I've always wanted to do that. Any other adventures?"

Robert sighs. "No, I'm a flatliner."

She gets this, smiles appreciatively. "What a terrible thing to say about yourself. A young man in his prime."

"Well, if you want to stretch a point."

She puts her hand gently on his forearm. At once forward and grandmotherly. "In his prime," she insists.

She leaves the hand there a second, long enough for him to feel the warmth of it. And a little tremor in the groin. He still can't figure this. She's leaning at him, smiling at him, giving him more heat than he expects. But all in this really innocent way, right out in public. Anyone can look over and see them chatting. Like they're old friends. If she does want something, he almost admires her directness. If she doesn't, he wonders how she survives carrying on like this. But hell, what could she want? They're in different parts of the business, completely.

Robert glances at her hand as she draws it away. Then at the curve of her shoulder, then her chest.

"Well, Kathy, I've got domestic politics to sort out. By the way, I'm an associate managing editor. One of three, I'm afraid. Good to meet you."

"Likewise, Robert. We'll talk again."

She says this as if it's a simple fact. Not to be disputed. He almost says, *We will?* Just to test her. Instead he nods vaguely, says, "Bye."

He walks back toward his office. Of course, he has to do what's best for the paper. Give the story to the best reporter for the job, the hell with that they want. Jesus, they're almost children, always squabbling, posturing, parading their egos. He sees her in his mind. This Kathy—what'd she say? Becker. Yeah, Becker. What, she's the friendliest woman in Manhattan? She's on happy pills? She's in heat? What? Funny thing. The mood was all wrong for the office. Suppose they were at a bar. The next step is you start necking, then go home. Yeah, the good old days. I can remember. Man, suppose I'm not happily married. I'd be curious, that's for sure.

He can still see her smile, a few feet in front of him. Damn. The kind of smile that says, Come on over here, and we'll do anything you want. Really, he thinks, that's what it said, right? What the hell?

Robert goes in his office, stares at the two reporters. "You guys still here?"

"You said to wait," one says petulantly.

"It's a joke, Armstrong. Alright, I'll tell you what's going down. Then there won't be any further discussion. Are we clear on that?"

They're staring at him. Usually so soft, so laid back, the big den mother, that's his style. They sense some change. Robert realizes his chest is a little tense, his pulse hammering away so he can feel it. Kathy Becker, huh? What the hell was all that?

Chapter 2

The train arrives right on time. 8:43 A.M. Robert moves along wth the thousand other commuters, through the huge space of Grand Central, down a large passageway, out onto East 42nd Street.

He wonders if he'll see her today. Let's see, Wednesday. Nothing this week so far. She's got this way of turning up unexpectedly, casually. Hey, it's the Big Editor! Yo, Big Rob, who's winning the newspaper wars? Hi, Robie, what's happening?

He smiles as he trudges along. The *New York News* building is two blocks up, on the right. A quick little commute down from Westchester, forty minutes door to door.

He's got a gray suit on, a big green parka over that, a soft brown stetson on his head. He walks along hunched over against the cold wind, hands in his pockets. It's a bright day but still the middle of winter. He notices dirty slush in the gutters, from the big storm a week ago.

Yeah, he thinks, she's due. Let's put some money down. A hundred dollars even money she shows. Yeah, I'll take that bet.

The woman's lively, he thinks. Got to give her that. Couldn't be from New York. You just know it. The amazing thing is she's really very pretty. But not that fine, delicate beauty that the models have. Something weak about that. Kathy's more robust. A down-to-earth, soap-and-water kind of beauty, he thinks. You don't imagine her at a fancy ball, making empty talk. Maybe on a horse, doing something. Hell, riding the south forty. Doesn't matter. Point is, she's capable, confident. A real easygoing way about her. What was it she said? Kicking ass and taking names. . . . Right. How's it going in marketing? I said. And she says, Oh, I'm kicking ass and taking names.

Robert Saunders laughs as he crosses Third Avenue.

Yeah, truth is, I hope she shows up. Makes me feel good.

Then he shudders, not from the cold. Thinking how crazy it is that he would flirt, no matter how harmlessly, with this woman. Why's she do it anyway? That's the question.

He's never had this problem before. Always sort of formal. A tough guy if he has to be. A woman's too friendly, you just don't notice. Hell, he thinks, it's like they say. L.A. is about money, New York is about work. People don't have time to mess around. You want messing around, go to the sticks. People bored out of their brains. Man, there's nothing to do but get in trouble.

He reaches the building, trudges straight across the big lobby, making it a point not to look around, not to check for her.

"Well, Big Bad Robie."

There she is. The voice ripples a thrill down his arms. But he keeps going a few steps, pretending not to hear her. Then, almost as an afterthought, he half turns. A little smile of recognition. Oh, you. Last thing I expected.

"Oh . . . Kathy." Like he can't even remember her name. "How're you doing?"

"Doing good, Big Rob. And you?" She gives him that hot little smile. Cool and knowing. Mischievous eyes.

But she stays a few feet from him. The way she holds herself is very guarded. Anybody seeing them would think they hardly know each other.

He just stares for a few seconds, pretending to be preoccupied, something else on his mind, looking at something else. Certainly not at the way her black hair waves down almost to her shoulders, not at the tendons in her white throat, not at the curve of her lips.

"Robie, my man," she pushes with her voice. "What's up in newspaper land?"

Robert shrugs, hunches his wide shoulders, his hands still down in his pockets. "Well," he says confidentially, "we in newspaper land are all atwitter this morning. Mayor's giving a press conference. Amazing man. He does something dumb. Then he says he didn't do it. Then he apologizes for doing it. Then he says this thing he didn't do, it was necessary to do it. And besides, he's appointing a commission to make sure it never happens again. Not that it ever did."

Kathy smiles. Hey, look at all the words she got out of him. "*Look out*, Dan Rather. Robie, they ought to put you on the tube."

Robert Saunders laughs. Playing the cool big brother. "Everything all right, Kathy?"

"Oh, sure."

"Good."

"You know," she says in a musing way, "that's something you could teach me about. Politics."

"Maybe," he says vaguely.

They reach the elevators, go into a crowded cab. They stop talking, pretend to ignore each other.

Chapter

3

"So run this by me again," Kathy says to her friend Louise. "He's nice or he isn't?" She sees the friend take out a cigarette. "Hey, give me one of those. I've quit."

"Me, too," Louise says, and they both laugh. "I only smoke after meals. And coffee. And sex. And when I really need one."

"Hell," Kathy says, "you *really* have quit, haven't you?!" She lights a Carlton and watches her friend through the smoke. They used to be real close. Oh, well. "So come on, Louise. What's he really getting at?" Talking about her ex.

"You?"

Kathy shrugs. "You have to figure."

"Where's he been the last year? I asked him, and he says, 'Around.'"

"Probably in jail," Kathy says. "Best place for him."

"You used to say he was a hell of a man." Louise pushes

her cup around, waits to see how Kathy will answer that. They're in a coffee shop near Fifth, people and traffic moving by outside the plate-glass window.

"Louise, heroin is a hell of a drug. Good luck."

"You and Keith did heroin?"

"If you can think it, we did it."

Louise blows smoke up, making a slow whistle. "Wow."

"Please. That was then, this is now."

"Oh, you think you've outgrown him?"

"I should hope so. Listen, I'm almost thirty-one. That three-oh messes with your head, let me tell you. And getting divorced. And something you don't know. Mom's been sick. Little stroke before Christmas. She's all right, but it makes you think. Dad bought it when I was young. Well, you know that."

"Terrible night."

"Yeah. Anyway, I thought Mom would be around forever. All of a sudden I'm looking at being the adult in the family."

Louise leans back in the chair, trying to act sophisticated, the way Kathy is acting. They used to raise such hell together. "You think you've outgrown me, too?"

Kathy grimaces. "Come on, Louise. I'm real busy. New job. I'm working real hard."

"Like it, huh?"

"Sure. I get it now. I used to think, *Who do these assholes think they are?* Now I know. They think they're bosses. I put myself in their place and I know exactly what they want. I do that plus a little more. Got to move on up, right?"

Louise watches her friend carefully. Kathy is different. The clothes, the makeup, the manner. Gone Manhattan. And there's something else. Not so tough? Happier? Got to be a man.

"Moving up in Manhattan," Louise says, a little sarcastically. They used to call themselves Jersey girls. Always sneered at the snobby bitches across the Hudson. "So who's the new man?"

Kathy laughs. “Whoa, now you’re a psychic. There’s no new man. Come on, talk about Keith. Run it through again. He didn’t threaten you, did he?”

“No, he just stood there with his insolent, fuck-you Elvis eyes. Got this motorcycle the size of a van.”

“Harley.”

“Right, a Harley waiting in front of my building. And the first thing he says is, ‘Hi, Louise. Still got the best bod in Jersey?’ ”

Kathy laughs. “Well?”

“Well what?”

“Do you?”

“Is this funny? The man’s a lunatic. According to you.”

“But you didn’t tell him anything. And he didn’t threaten you. Or did he?”

“He’s a threat standing there. Looks me up and down, then side to side—”

“Does he ever mention me by name?”

“Once. ‘So how’s Kathy?’ Something like that.”

“Louise. Please listen to me.” Kathy rubs out the cigarette, then leans over the table. “Don’t play games with him. Don’t talk to him. Just call the police. Period.”

“Like you said, he’s a hell of a man.”

“Pleeeasse. Hey, you want to get out of here? Got enough?”

“Yeah, sure.”

Kathy places a ten and a five on the check. They put on their coats and walk outside into the cold afternoon.

“I just broke up,” Louise says. “Or I think I did. I’m a little tender.”

They walk along 43rd toward Fifth. “I get it,” Kathy says. “My ex looks like a little excitement. Believe me, that’s the way he sees himself. Mr. Excitement. Look, all I ask, please don’t help him find me. Nothing. Other than that, you’re on your own. You want somebody to fuck you for three hours and then say, ‘See ya, bitch,’ go ahead.”

Louise laughs. “Three hours?”

"The shit we did! I tell you now, you'll be dripping in the street. I tell you, Louise, he's probably been running drugs. If I'd stayed with him, he'd have me robbing banks."

"How close did you get?"

"We were in Cleveland, then Cincinnati. Talked about it some. I think he's joking. He's not. Keith's not much for jokes. The things you think are jokes are usually something real important to him."

The two women walk around the corner onto Fifth. There's a big crowd of people half a block up. An ambulance is backing slowly into the crowd.

"What the hell?" Kathy says. "Somebody got mugged right on Fifth Avenue?"

"This city! Makes me scared."

They push into the edge of the crowd. Kathy can just make out a body sprawled on the curb. "Makes me mad."

"Why do you want to live here?"

"Big leagues, it's still the big leagues." Kathy nudges a man. "What happened?"

He shrugs. "I didn't see it. Car got out of control, ran up on the sidewalk. Got two people."

"See," Kathy tells Louise, "not a mugging, after all."

"Same crazy city. Get you one way or the other."

Kathy takes her friend's arm. "Come on." They walk on toward 42nd. The big library across the street. "Could happen anywhere."

Louise studies the other woman. More composed than she remembers. "I got it," Louise announces.

"What?"

"The reason you won't tell me about the new man."

"What?"

"He's married."

Kathy stops and faces her friend. Smiling. They're on 42nd now, the sun slanting down on them. "I've got some plans. That's all I'll tell you. Might jinx it."

"Oh, don't do it, Kath. Date a married man? Are you crazy?

Never works. They never leave their wives."

Kathy stops smiling. "Oh, you think I could be some guy's plaything? A little girl lost in the big city? You think that, Louise?"

Louise is taken aback. "*Hey!* I'm just worried about you."

"Yeah, well, good. But don't think I'm stupid. I'm not." She softens, pats Louise's arm. "Fact is, the more I hang around here, I realize I'm pretty damned smart. The thing is, Lou, you just have to get in the game and play. Then you find out all the other people are pretty ordinary. Come on, let's lighten up. Walk me back to work. I'll pay your cab back to Hoboken. Fair? Really, I appreciate you coming over here. And don't even think about messing with Keith."

Kathy laughs to herself.

"What?" Louise asks.

"Just thinking. Look, I'm not apologizing for anything I've done. Screw it. I'm not ashamed of anything. That doesn't mean I want to do it over. I don't want to be twenty again. Not even twenty-eight. I've got a new life. I think it'll be a good one."

Kathy stops herself. No point in bragging, making her friend jealous. But yeah, when she thinks about it, when she looks ahead, things look real good. No guarantees, everyone knows that. But hell, things look good.

Louise is staring at her. Head tilted a little. Questioning maybe. Doubting.

"Louise, listen. You've got good instincts. Being a nurse must do that. Yeah, there's a married man. But he's not *that* married. One of those dead-end marriages."

Louise challenges her. "How do you know that?"

"Hey, married eight years, no kids. What's that tell you? Look, I've seen them together, some big office party, before Christmas. No chemistry. So what's the point?" Kathy shrugs, smiling intently at Louise. "No point! I really think I'm doing her a favor. She'll get somebody more, you know, *suitable.*

Then we'll have four happy people. The way it ought to be, right? Anyway, my guy deserves a lot more."

Louise laughs nervously. "You?"

"Oh, you know more than that?"

Louise starts to argue. "No, sweetie, put it here." She raises her hand for Kathy to slap. They laugh, then they hug. "Good luck, girlfriend." Louise smiles bravely. "I'll keep Keith away."

"Shoot him. He understands that. Man loves guns."

Louise stares at her old friend. Her face confused. "You really don't miss him? Come on, Kathy. Really?"

"Another life, Louise. We were married four years and I want to forget all but maybe a week."

"One great week, huh?"

"Spread over four years? Nothing great about it."

They laugh some more, crossing Fifth Avenue.

Chapter 4

Robert and his wife, Anne, go out to dinner with another couple, Sam and Marie. They're good friends. He's a stockbroker, she's in banking. A pleasant, normal evening. Robert finds it reassuring. Everything in its place. And a long way from the craziness of Manhattan. And from Kathy.

The wives go to the bathroom and Sam says, "You got any problems? No, you don't. *I* took forty thousand of my own money up to three hundred thou, trading options. Losing it all as we sit here. I tell you, man, I go to work like it's death row."

"Damn," Robert says, "the whole three hundred thousand? Gone?"

"Hell no. There's fifty or sixty dollars left." The other man laughs grimly. "And you know what? Marie cuts out coupons. She takes me to the grocery, tells me, 'Look, dear,

I just saved twelve dollars.' Hard not to strangle her, right there."

"You can't tell her about the options, huh?"

"You kidding? She just saved twelve dollars! Another world. . . . I *live* to trade. She couldn't understand. Heck, neither could the SEC."

The two couples say good night in front of the restaurant. A chilly, moonless night. Robert stares at Sam's wife. Sam made a fortune, lost a fortune. She doesn't know word one. It feels strange, somehow lonely, to Robert. That he should know something so personal and she doesn't. He almost wishes Sam hadn't told him. It changed the mood.

Then, as they're driving home, Anne puts her face in her hands and starts crying. Robert stares disbelieving at the side of her face. His first reaction is guilt. Something he did, said, thought. . . . How could Anne know? Jesus, just one drink, Anne, that's all we did. Politics, we talked—

"Oh, Robert, I'm sorry."

"Anne . . . what is it?" He drives with one hand, patting her back nervously with the other.

"Oh, nothing, really. Something at work."

Robert sighs, a pleasurable feeling of relief. "Oh well, *tell* me about it. Damn. Don't keep it to yourself."

"It's nothing, really. There's a lot of stress. You know that promotion . . . ?"

"Yes?"

"I'm just sure I won't get it."

"Now . . . you deserve that."

"Office politics." She wipes her eyes, smiles bravely. Turning more toward Robert. He presses harder on her back. "Marie was just telling me how much she wants to have children. Sam hates the thought. He actually hates children. Isn't that strange? I felt so sorry for her. You like children, don't you? I mean, really like them?"

"Yes, I do. I really do. Whenever you're ready . . ."

"I tell you, some days at work, I think, drop it, go home, get pregnant."

They're driving a winding, back road. Not much light. Houses hard to see. Abruptly a streetlamp shines on Anne's face. Robert can see the streaked makeup. She sniffs a little. He wants to help her, comfort her. . . . Damn. She gets upset too easily. Anne! Come on, be tougher.

Was she always like this? Age is scaring her? The career is too much? Robert isn't sure. She always had a certain reserve, a prim quality. But he thought of it as good breeding, as responsible, adult behavior. Things he thought he wanted in his own life. Maybe he's seeing her a different way now, asking for more. Maybe she hasn't changed at all. But he's seeing her as too well bred, too mature, too fussy.

He glances at his wife, watches her wipe her face. He can't imagine Kathy acting like this. He thinks of Kathy's easy manner, how she seems in control of things. Character, gumption, sass—whatever you want to call it, Robert thinks she's got it. Thank God. So many unhappy people in Manhattan, all whining about one thing or the other. Hard to imagine sometimes how the country ever got built.

Anne snuggles closer. "You're a good man, Robert."

He hugs her with his right arm, smiling uneasily. She rubs his thigh. In that tentative way she has. He never knows whether they're going to do something or they're not. It never seems quite right to say, "Damn it, Anne, are we screwing or aren't we?"

He reaches their street, then the driveway. Turns the motor off. "Come on, honey. We'll get a nightcap. Something real expensive. You'll feel better."

She puts her arms around his neck, leans on him. "Sorry I'm so silly tonight. It's just a bad day."

Robert studies her face. She's pretty in a sensible, no-nonsense way. The blond hair not too long, permed close to her head. Blond? Mousey is more like it. God, that's it, we don't even have kids, but Anne looks just the way a boy wants his mother to look. Nice but not too sexy.

Robert kisses her nose, then turns to open the car door. Yeah, he thinks, they say you marry a woman like your mother. Or you marry your mother, deep down? How's that go? Never mind. What a downer.

He unlocks the front door to their house. Aware of Anne standing close to him. Maybe they are doing something. Yeah, he wants to. But he's got this dread, already, that he'll fantasize about Kathy. Won't be able to stop himself. But he'll feel guilty and, what the hell, the next thing you know, he'll lose it. . . . Maybe *two* nightcaps.

"Oh, it's so beautiful and cold out here," Anne says behind him. "Look at it, Robert. All the stars."

He turns around to look at the sky. Then, off to his right, he notices the huge red glow of Manhattan. Hot and sexy. He wonders what Kathy is doing. . . .

He looks back toward Anne. Oh, damn, he thinks, she's going to dance around on the lawn. Fucking stars just make me feel small. Shrivel a guy's dick permanently. He remembers how morbid he could get at sixteen, looking up at the stars. Knowing they'd still be in the same spots when he was dead, and his children were dead, and their children. Fucking stars.

Anne runs back to him, pushing him through the open front door. "So," she says, in the accent she uses when she feels playful, "you are feeling perhaps wild and crazy tonight, young man?"

Robert laughs. "How'd you know?"

They go into the foyer. "Robert," she exclaims, "hold me." She leans against him and his big hands press against her back. Anne looks up at him. "You're so reassuring," she says.

This makes him shrug awkwardly. He grins.

Anne says in a girlish voice, "You did mention the good stuff? The twenty-year-old port perhaps."

"Oh, yeah, great," Robert says.

She stands on her toes, kisses him solemnly on the mouth. Robert stares at her through half-shut eyes. But she's so nice, he thinks. Anne is so nice. *The perfect wife.* I always said that, didn't I?

"You're not tired," she says, "are you?"

"Oh, no, wide awake."

"And raring to go," Anne says, with a sweet nervous smile, as if she's said something outrageous.

Chapter 5

Robert sits in the back of the place, the one Kathy found. It's just off Lex, six blocks below where they work. Better than a dive, but not the kind of place other editors would go. "A good safe place," Kathy said. Just hearing the word *safe* made him feel uneasy, guilty.

He's in a booth, staring at the front, watching, waiting. She's a few minutes late. The first time they did this she was there ahead of him. He came in, saw her, it felt good. Now he has time to think, worry. He stares furtively at each of the people walking in the door, or walking by him. Does he know them? Could anybody recognize him? Does it make any difference? The light is very low. Still, he keeps the parka on, sitting there with his arms on the table, his shoulders hunched up to cover part of his face. He feels obvious, conspicuous. He always laughed at people sneaking out of porno stores or cruising the hookers on Tenth. Hell, he thought, if I do that, I'm not hiding. Bullshit. The more hiding the better, that's how he sees it now.

You don't see anybody you know for years. Naturally he'd see someone here, now. *Hey, Rob, how's Anne? You alone? Can I join you?* The obnoxious little scenario unrolls in his head. *What's up? You're not waiting for somebody, are you? Business, Rob? Hey, you're not . . . running around, are you?* . . . Robert imagines snatching the guy up, throwing him over the bar. A little late. He knows. Everybody knows.

Robert looks at his fingers, realizes he's tapping the table. His body feels tense, his mouth dry. He hates waiting anyway. But now he's waiting for Kathy, and they're bound to be discovered, and besides they don't have that much time.

Just a little meeting, pretend it's casual, no big deal, doesn't mean anything. Well, what the hell does it mean?

"Jesus," he mutters.

I just wish she'd come in the door. That smile. The way she glides in, a little cocky, a little flirtatious. Dressed up in a nice, elegant way, one of those executive outfits. But you don't forget it's a woman inside there. Not for a second. Oh, she makes sure of that.

That's the thing. She's running this whole game? Controlling it? Feels like that sometimes. But for what? Love, lust, getting ahead? Or she's this little girl falling for the big editor? Maybe a *Cosmo* girl, doing what that dumb magazine tells her to do, try some new adventure. Maybe she's just friendly. Maybe she doesn't fucking *know*. Damn it.

Robert feels the insanity of being here. Drifting out of work a little early. Making excuses. Hell, *lying*. Trying to look invisible. Hoping nobody notices when he walks south instead of toward Grand Central. And for what? So he can sit across the table from her for a half hour?

Jesus. Am I crazy?

Ahhhhh. He sees her framed in the doorway. Fifty feet away, he can feel the heat of her, the joy. God, what a rush. He sits up straighter, stares at her, can't help smiling.

Come on, baby. Come on down here. I'm waiting just for you. . . .

•••

Not much time left, if he's going to catch the 6:04. Finally Robert says, "So why are we here?"

That's good, she thinks. Either the dumbest question she's ever heard, or the smartest.

She lets a few seconds go by. Then she makes a little shrug, answers in a low, sincere voice. "You have to ask?"

Impulsively, her hands reach out, take one of his. The first time they've touched. He tries not to notice, not to gasp. He thinks his hand will catch fire.

A tremor starts up from his left knee, stalks through his genitals and skids to a stop in the skin of his belly. Lovely and scary.

"Damn," he says aloud but softly. Trying to be casual. "Nice hands."

She laughs, squeezes his hand tighter. "That's my line."

I've got a hard-on, he thinks, and I feel exactly like I'm sixteen. It was *just like this.* All hot glands and awkward everything. What do you do? What do you say? That's just it. You never know. You just sit there with your tongue hanging out, and your dick sticking up, and you don't know what the hell you're supposed to do. Or what you want to do. Or how you feel.

He struggles for some middle ground, no cheap jokes, no wild declarations. He wants to say, "This is a little, uh, unsettling for me." Too wimpy? Instead he says, "You look real nice."

She nods, smiling in a serious way. Showing him she understands what he's feeling, that she's patient. Moving her fingers slightly, caressing the back of his hand.

He glances down, sure there'll be burn marks where she's touching him. Actual red marks. No, his hands look completely ordinary. But the tingling, the electricity, going up and down his arm is astonishing. But what is it really? Desire? Wonderful, idiot desire? Or some weird playing with danger? Something he shouldn't have, so he desires it more? And this desire, being so strong, so mixed up with guilt, seems more valid than any other thought or emotion? If he were single, if he could lean over and casually kiss her, would he feel even half of it?

"This is nice," Robert says, taking her hands briefly between his. "But it's getting late. If I start now, I can walk it. Like I said," he smiles, "you're looking real nice."

He gets out his wallet, puts a ten on the table for their drinks.

Kathy says, "I think it'll be all right to leave with you." There, that conspiratorial note. She's good at letting it slip in now and then. They're in this together. In deep.

They stand up and move toward the door. She walks a half step behind him. He feels her fingers lightly clutching his elbow, or tickling it. A little secret communication: I'm here.

Yeah, Robert thinks, like I'm going to forget.

He pushes through the door, goes out onto East 36th, glancing nervously at the people walking by.

Chapter

6

Anne Saunders stares from one big monitor to the other, spread sheets on both screens. She leans back in her chair, glances at the clock on the wall, sighs, plays with a pencil.

Yeah, *clock*, she thinks. My clock. What time is it? It's late.

The rows of figures blur. This company's books are so unbalanced, she knows she'll be struggling the rest of the day to put them in order.

Robert, she thinks, seems not quite himself . . . or perhaps I'm more needful. Probably it's my fault. Oh yes, definitely. . . . The job's not so challenging anymore. But I *want* that promotion. . . . The possibility of children floats before her mind, very real, and she scans the terrain for dangers to this idea. . . . I'm so sensitive to the little pluses and minuses. You think about the problems and you're overwhelmed. It's a wonder anybody has children.

A knock on the door. She turns and sees Edd—"that's two

d's"—Lawrence. "Hi, how're you doing? Eating in? Want to try the cafeteria with me?"

She stares at his bland, pleasant face. Just the sort of man who makes everyone think tax people are dull. The most interesting thing about him, she thinks, is the two d's.

"Oh, sure, Edd. I'm having a rough morning with Smithers, Inc."

"Oh, well," Edd says casually, "just throw the IRS a VP, they'll be happy."

Anne frowns. Not exactly the way she sees her job.

She shuts the door to her office, and they walk down to the elevators.

"The IRS usually wants money," she says. "Or does the VP trick work for you?"

"Just kidding," he says with no smile. "But, hey, the books are a mess, maybe somebody's been cooking."

"I hope not. I think it's just a case of people finding more tax gimmicks than a corporate body can digest."

"Ah, the Eighties. I miss 'em."

They go up to 12, where the firm has a swank little cafeteria. The idea being to keep the drudges in the building. Anne takes the fish and salad. Edd takes the burger, fries, red jello, and chocolate mousse cake. As they're sitting down, Anne says, "You in training?"

Edd doesn't see the joke, or won't acknowledge it. "They make a good burger here." He's lean, almost stiff in his movements, wearing a navy-blue suit and white shirt. Close to her age, Anne thinks.

"Right." She smiles briefly. "So what's new with you?"

Edd shrugs. "Well, I keep getting more master points. You don't play bridge, do you?"

"Not well."

"I remember. Scrabble's your game."

"Used to play it all the time. Robert's a managing editor now and, in practical terms, that means he doesn't have time for things like Scrabble."

"There's no way out," Edd says.

"Well, you play bridge."

"My wife left me for that very reason."

Anne smiles. An odd, no-nonsense man. One could well imagine a wife leaving him. Still, he doesn't seem to have any pretensions. Or he has the secret kind that are more fun because nobody knows about them.

A group of young lawyers, all men, come in. Only one has a jacket on. They all wear wide suspenders. They're high spirited and settle noisily at a nearby table, three facing three. Edd glances at them without interest. Anne looks more closely. They make her appreciate Robert. They're all around thirty, but still boys. Nobody wants to grow up these days. They're vital, attractive; but Anne feels something almost maternal toward them.

They trade jokes in low voices, laugh a lot, then start comparing cases and tactics. "All right," one says loudly, "listen to this. The burglar gets the window open, gets his leg in. The guy in the house, he comes running. Says stop or get out or something. The guy in the window has a tool or makes a move or something. The homeowner shoots him. The guy falls back on the lawn. Wounded bad but he lives. What happens?"

"Witnesses say what?"

"Only one. A house away, in the dark. He can't say how far the guy was in the window. If he was. Or what was said. If anything."

"I'll take it." A slim one with slicked-back hair pauses for effect. Anne thinks his name is Stan. He raises his hands, about to paint a picture. "This guy's drunk, says he is. Alright, go with me. He thinks it's his house. Lost his key. He went around back, tries to get in through a window."

"Come on," another says, "the houses have to look alike."

"He's real drunk. Any medical evidence to the contrary?"

"Nope. ER treated for gunshot. Why check blood alcohol?"

"There you go. Guy's really drunk. He's lost. Or maybe it's

a friend's house, guy he knows always leaves a window open. Never mind. He's no burglar. Last thing on his mind."

"Bingo," says the guy giving the case. "What else?"

"Now it's a piece of cake," another says. "Mainly, he never was inside. Guy who shot him is guilty of assault, attempted murder, reckless endangerment, all that good stuff. Wounded guy can sue the homeowner for everything he's got. Wounded guy's wife can sue for loss of services."

"That's what I'm doing. Wounded guy—get this—has enough presence to drag himself a yard or two away from the house. Guy's done time, learned a lot of law. Police records show him ten feet away. Guy in the house clearly overreacted, used unnecessary force. Probably a gun nut. He could get a few."

Anne can't believe this. "Wait a minute," she breaks in from eight feet away, "you're representing the burglar?"

"Alleged."

They all laugh, staring at Anne.

"But he's probably got a record."

"Huge. But inadmissable."

"And you know he's lying?"

That gets a lot of hoots. The slim one named Stan says, "Hey, it's just a game."

Anne stands up with her tray. "You're helping the burglar sue the . . . the victim?"

Stan smiles up at Anne. In a courtly cowboy accent, he says, "Begging your pardon, ma'am, but victims are shit."

All the young men laugh at the profound cynicism of that.

"Seriously," another says, "it's pro-bono work. The firm has to have a conscience, that's what the senior partner says." All of them grinning at that.

Edd stands up, too. "We're in the tax end, fellows. We don't get to see the juicy stuff."

They all smile happily. Yeah, the juicy stuff. That's what they get to see all day.

"Isn't that disgusting," Anne says as they leave the cafeteria.

"What we do with numbers, they do with people."

"Please, Edd. I'm a little more sentimental about my work, if you don't mind."

"Of course I don't mind. But you know how the system works. All you can do is stay away from it."

Anne waves a hand. "I'm sorry, I don't like the way they were talking."

Edd shrugs and they go back to their floor in silence. In front of her office, he says, "Thanks, Anne. I appreciate the company." And he wanders on down the hall.

Anne goes in her office. For a minute she stands by her big window, which looks over White Plains. A sliver of the Hudson River in the distance. Bright gray sky. The sun breaking through here and there. Last week of February. Psychologically, Anne thinks, winter's over when we get to March.

Alright, she thinks, maybe I did react too strongly. Something about those boys; I was thinking about being their mother, and suddenly I don't like my sons.

She smiles and turns back to her desk, staring blankly at the two screens.

Or I'm more on edge than I think. This whole ticking clock thing is a weight. The promotion is probably out of my reach. Damn it all but okay. Is there something else? She sees Robert in her mind. Always working very hard. A little distracted maybe. Is something different? What would it be?

No, she thinks, it's probably me. It's my fault. Definitely.

I always worry too much. More than Robert anyway. It was always like that. He could be silly, and I tried to learn from him. Right from the first date, it was like that. All my life, I got straight A's, obeyed all the rules. "Sometimes," Robert said, "you have to say, 'Screw the rules.' " It sounded so daring.

She remembers a night before they married, at a bowling alley, drinking too many beers, acting like kids. A *lot* of gutter balls! . . . She smiles thinking about the snapshots they got from a machine, four for a dollar. Their heads pressed ear to ear, grinning, mugging for the camera. The snaps are in a scrapbook somewhere, but she doesn't need to have them before her. She can see the expressions exactly. We look so young, she thinks, and so happy. Robert taught me how. . . .

Oh well, she sighs, you get older, the worries pile up. Can't stay young forever, no matter how hard you try. Ouch! She thinks again of the ticking clock. Yeah, we've really got to deal with that. Is it baby time? Is that what I really want? Are we ready?

Anne shakes her thoughts back to work. She points her pencil at a row of numbers on the screen. "*Just* a million seven out of whack. Sure, let's trade a VP." She smiles, thinking of Edd's curiously blank manner. Funny, someone more grown up than I am.

She focuses on the numbers, goes back to work.

Chapter 7

The cabbie comes across East 40th. Racing and braking, playing his private games with rush-hour traffic. Sees a hand shoot up on the left, brakes hard toward the curb. He rolls just past, gets a good look at the figure inside the raincoat, shudders his shoulders by way of approval. Then she's in the back, leaning right up to the partition, kind of shouting, "Turn up Third. Get on the right. We'll pick somebody up at 44th Street."

He sees her in his mirror. A real looker with black hair, hot red lipstick, bright eyes, something tough around the mouth. He shoots over to Third, swings wide onto the avenue. In the mirror he sees she's put on some fancy sunglasses, sort of Hollywood. She's in the middle of the seat, staring up ahead.

"There," she shouts, "tall man in a dark coat."

Cabbie pulls over and this fairly big guy opens the door and quickly stoops down to get in. Smart-looking, might be an exec . . . no, more like an architect. Maybe a little tense today. Don't worry, buddy. She'll fix you up.

"Just drive up to the park, drive around," the woman says through the clear plastic partition. Then she moves to the left and sits staring straight ahead, as if she hardly knows the guy.

A little weird, the cabbie thinks. He grabs his clipboard, pretends to write something, hears the woman say softly, "Hi, big guy."

The big guy's staying by the right door, also staring ahead.

"Let's *go*," the woman shouts.

The cabbie hits the gas, thinking, Head up to the park, huh? Ride around, huh? Hey, no fucking in the cab, okay? Just kidding. An extra ten'll take care of it. I won't even look. Much.

He works into the middle of Third, gets up near 50th Street, then shifts around in his seat some, get the best angle on these two. She's more in the center now, facing the guy. Nice profile. Great smile. He's leaning to her, getting that big head down closer. Seems she's holding his arm now. Talk, talk, talk. Yeah, well, talk louder! Hell, with the motor, the wind, I can't hear a damned word.

Cabbie catches a light on 54th. Good. See what's happening here. He thinks he's seen this, people pretending not to know each other, at least not real well. Then you get moving, and they go at it. So what've you got? Not a married couple. When are they all over each other? Haha. Alright, they do it now and then. But they don't act cold at the start. Right? Right.

Cabbie leans his head back on the partition, like a tired guy. Makes a show of staring up at the light. ". . . thinking about you all day," he hears the woman say. "You devil." Then silence. Ohhh, kissy, kissy sounds. Cabbie grabs his crotch. Be still, my dick.

Light changes and the cabbie speeds up to 59th, turns left and goes across toward Sixth. Yeah, if the lady has another idea, I know she'll speak *right up.* Geez, some of these dames these days.

Lots of traffic on Central Park South. The horse carriages all lined up. One of his favorite streets. The park still bare. Fucking winter, get outta here.

Problem now, he thinks, is sitting a little higher, get a look down, see what they're doing. He shifts around, flexes his shoulders, do that seventh-inning stretch sitting down. As he turns right into the park, he gets a good look. Whoa, they're locked! Let's see, who's groping who here? She's got an arm around his neck, the other hand in his jacket, rubbing his chest. All right, keeping it clean. And this guy is kissing her ear, *holy shit—tongue!* I need a drink—

Almost sideswipes a brand-new Lexus, instantly rolls the window down a few more inches, shouts, "Hey, pal, learn to drive. And buy American, you asshole!"

Cabbie wants desperately to turn around, look at them all at once, instead of little pieces at a time. He's on the drive now, heading northeast. Cars on each side of him. Little tricky in here. No good stomping some fucking Japobile. The paperwork'll kill ya. Need a stoplight.

The light's red near 72nd Street. The traffic real thick. More than a dozen cars stopped ahead of him. Bicyclists weaving past his door. Goddamned kids on skateboards taking his paint off.

Hey, I open the door in your face, see how you like that. Alright, let's see, the left hand's on her neck. In the hair, looks like. Hey, put me in there, coach. Now, that right hand. Down there somewhere. Oh shit, can't see. . . . Guy's face, let's see? Still tense. God, he's going crazy. But having fun? Whoa, there it is! A ring the size of a ball and chain.

The cabbie gulps trying not to laugh. Oh, well, excuse me, Nookie Man, but did you get permission?

The meter trips to $9. Cabbie thinks, Great, ride this park all day. No, they probably don't have much time. I'll just drive like a bat, run this thing way up.

The light changes and the traffic curves left, then right, heading north. Cabbie gets the speed up to 55, 60, slicing through the clear March chill.

He looks in the mirror again, realizes they've shifted left, more behind him. Fuck is this? What, they saw him? Trying to hide? The back of the guy's head is in the center of his mirror. To see her, he leans hard up against the door. Geez, he wants to adjust the mirror. But maybe they're watching him. Hey, you pervert. Who, moi? Fuck you, buddy, never saw you fuck her, besides your technique needs work.

Cabbie laughs a little to himself, thinking, No, it's not him saw me. Guy's got enough on his mind. It's her. Bitch. Mind your own business, lady. Guy driving a cab *has* to use the rearview mirror. It's the fucking law.

Hey, maybe they're just *lying down more.* Don't care about me one way or another. Wow. Yeah, like she's sinking down, getting him on her. Like she's overcome by the hots. I don't know, babe. You that hot? Fuck this, I'm that hot. He's got his hand on your tits, I'll die. Crash this fucking thing and go to heaven.

Cabbie figures a way. Gets in the left lane, waits, then steers suddenly to the right, so he has to look back over his shoulder, check traffic. Check that skirt almost up to there. Oh, sweet Jesus. Guy's right hand in the blouse, just the back of his wrist showing. I'm dying. It's not worth it. Meter's tripping $14. Who cares? *I'm paying*. Hey, folks, maybe we can do this regular.

Cabbie stares grimly ahead, hunches over the wheel. Reaches down to rub his hard-on. Thinking how pretty she is. What are those breasts? . . . 36C probably. Hell, make 'em D. More for me. Hey, I got the dreams, guy's got the nipple. I *know* it. Like a grape. Go ahead, get it out, suck it. I won't look. Much!

A horn blasts through his head. He looks at the road, sees he's over the yellow line, a few inches from another car. Scary! He ignores the guy, coolly steers back to his lane.

"Sorry, folks," the cabbie yells toward the back seat. "Lot of jerks on the road."

Hey, don't mind me, you two just go right ahead. Me, I'm having safe sex up here. Hey, if you can call safe having some fuck trying to run you off the road. Cabbie smiles, wondering if he could reach out and adjust the outside mirror, maybe see her that way. Jesus, I'm a nervous wreck up here. Always fuck the workingman, even when they *don't.* Isn't it the truth? Hey, *fuck* this workingman!

They're near the top of the park now, a twisting, hilly stretch. Stay alert, buddy. Some kids with a rock could try to steal my love birds. No fucking way, José. I'm bringing the goods home. Which is more than I can say for Mister-Don't-Let-Your-Meatloaf here.

Fuck it, the cabbie thinks. He rolls down his window, fiddles with the mirror, peers hard, gets a nice shot of mouths pressed together. Then they pull apart an inch, and the guy says something soulful, to judge by the serious expression. Guy looks like he wants something bad. *What*'s another question.

Oh, and that kisser on her. Those eyes. What'd that guy say in the army? Talking about his fiancée, girl back home, for Chrissake. Shows me this Polaroid, says, I'd crawl three miles over broken glass to hear this girl piss over the phone. Man, I almost fell on the floor. Now I got her in the back seat.

Man, look at the money I'm making. What the hell. I'll have to spend it all in some bar getting over this. I'm not looking *nooooo* more. That's it. Stress'll kill you.

Chapter 8

On Saturday, after lunch, Kathy takes a cab to Grand Central, catches the train up to the stop just south of Bronxville. Not taking any chances at all. She's got on a green raincoat she hasn't worn in years, a dark scarf over her hair, and her sunglasses. She finds a cab, gives the driver an address about a block away from Robie's house. She has to see it, see how he lives, see how she's going to live.

Robie was paying for drinks, and she said, "Oh, let me see your wallet. I want to see what kinds of things you have in there." She made a big deal out of the funny photo on his license. Then she had his address, without asking for it.

She sits back in the right corner of the cab. Enjoying the ride, the small roads, the great-looking homes they pass. She bought a map, knows generally where she is, how long the ride will take. Ah, Bronxville, she thinks, where I belong. And I had to be born in the ass end of Trenton.

And she's enjoying the suspense—maybe she'll see Robie. Maybe she'll see his wife.

Kathy's face tightens. Probably the wife is a nice enough woman, even if dull, plain, barren, and in the way. Just a stupid, lucky accident she got Robie. They do *not* belong together. Kathy doesn't want to let herself be emotional and thus perhaps careless. This is business, you might say. But that woman is all wrong for Robie. Kathy suspected this. Now she *knows* it. No, the fate of it—the plain common sense, really—is that she and Robie marry, have a number of children, and live happily and prosperously ever after. Good for each other the whole time.

Robie already knows what she wants, deep down. Watching the street signs flicker by, she wonders if she overplayed her hand. He asked about her marriage and Kathy told him about the dumb mistake she made, the uninteresting husband she got. Then she went a step too far, maybe. She looked in Robie's eyes and said, "Really, I just outgrew him. So I did what I had to do. I walked away from the marriage." A little challenge in her eyes. A little too much? Telling Robie, Hey, I did it, you can, too. All it takes is balls.

Yeah, balls. She smiles. That's all Robie needs to bring to the table. Everything else is taken care of.

Funny, she thinks, talking about Keith as dull, uninteresting. He was never any of that. Mr. Balls himself. Hey, no reason to threaten Robie. . . .

Actually, Keith was a fascinating guy, she thinks. Give him credit. But everything I want to get away from, leave far behind.

And hello to this. . . . The cab is close to Robie's neighborhood now. If she remembers right, this street intersects with his. Pretty homes everywhere Kathy looks. Not rich people. Upper middle class. Probably half-acre lots, maybe a full acre here and there. Plenty of space. Deep backyards. Two-story homes, ranch homes. Grass, kids, cars, bikes, mailboxes, trees, shrubs. Normal people, leading normal lives. People here, she thinks, they ought to get down on their knees every day, kiss the ground, thank the Lord, something. Hell, they probably bitch all the time they don't have it better. Not me. God, are you listening? Please, give me Robie, give me this. That's it. You won't hear a word out of me for the next fifty years. I won't look at another man. I'll raise good kids. Join the PTA. The whole thing. And not a peep out of me. That a deal, God? Please! I'll do my part, I promise!

Kathy sees the name of Robie's street. Her breathing quickens, which surprises her. She strains to pick out a number, figure how far away the house is. Let's see, oh, they're almost there. Jesus. The house is on her right—fifty feet outside the cab window. Just a low hedge separating them. Kathy presses herself back in the corner, peeks out. Nobody in sight. The cab is slowing, the guy looking for a number that actually doesn't exist. Robie's house is smallish, two stories. Well, hell, big for two people. White and a Colonial blue on the trim. Drive and garage to the right. Then a little fence with a row of small trees separating Robie's house from the nearest neighbor. Must be a backyard. . . .

The cab slows almost to a stop three houses up. "Keep going," Kathy snaps. "Don't stop."

The driver goes on up the street, waiting, frowning.

Kathy leans forward, smiling. "I'm house hunting. Let's turn around and go down this street real slow." Yeah, house hunting, she thinks. True, in a way.

Now she'll be on the opposite side, hidden inside the dark of the cab. No way anyone could glance out a window and see her.

As they come back, Kathy whispers, "Slow . . . slow in here." Her eyes jumping from window to window, looking for clues to Robie's life. Then she gets a one-second view of the back, sees a figure well behind the house. Robie, the wife? Kathy's not sure. One of them. Maybe talking to the other, who's closer to the house. So there they are.

Funny, she thinks, the reality doesn't depress me. I thought it might. No, it makes me surer. It's there, it's mine. Just a matter of time.

"Okay," she says, "we can go back to the station."

"To take the train? Bronxville is closer."

"Oh, no thanks. I've got friends who expect me in Mount Vernon." Trying to be calm, normal. So this guy won't remember she was in his cab. She was never here, never saw Robie's life.

Oh, someday I'll tell him. She smiles. He'll like it.

She feels very calm now. Feels good. Nice day. Just a matter of time.

Chapter 9

A hall on the 29th floor. Past the restrooms. Then there's a sharp turn and a door that goes out on a little landing, sort of recessed. A lot of old Manhattan office buildings have these. Robert stands there looking down at the city, the East River. Wearing an overcoat; the air temperature feels about 45. His windpipe is tight, his heart beating heavily. Just to touch her, that's *all* he wants. Which sounds even crazier when he thinks it.

Kathy eases past the heavy door. A stillness about her that seems to make him more excited. Hands in her coat pockets, head a little to the side. Smiling at him. Slowly she unbuttons her coat, holds it open. Twists a little, swells her chest. "Hi, big guy. . . . All yours."

He thinks of grabbing her hard, mauling her in his arms, sitting her on the railing, getting between her thighs. Not things he can so easily do. The city all around them, maybe somebody noticing them just this second. The guilt! Anne jumping into his head. And his staff down on 16 probably wondering where he is. He steps to her, slides his arms around her back, presses her against him.

"Silly me," he says, smiling awkwardly. "I've got a paper to put together. And all I can think about is . . . one kiss. From you."

They kiss for a long time. "Only one kiss?" she asks. She can see the tension in his face, feel the rigidity in his body. Partly it flatters her, partly it charms her, partly it amuses her. "You know what I told you. . . . I'm always here for you. Use me." She slides her palm down over the front of his pants. "Feels like a big dick to me. You think anybody's watching?" Robert stares wildly around. "Doesn't matter. All they see is two people talking." She unzips his pants, takes his prick out, strokes him firmly, not too quickly.

"What," he gasps.

She puts her lips close to his. "I'm jerking you off."

"But . . . ?"

"Oh? All that stuff? Hmmmm. Gallons of nice come. You better figure something out, lover."

Robert searches his pockets, almost desperately, comes up with two wrinkled napkins, put there at some long-ago restaurant or cocktail party. His legs are aching, and his groin is tightening. He positions the napkins just over his prick, with his left hand. He grips her shoulder with the other. "Oh, Kathy . . . I'm sorry . . . I didn't mean it to be like . . ."

She smiles, almost laughing at him. "Robie, darling. I'm yours. Besides, I like jerking you off. Feels great. How do you feel? Throbbing maybe?"

"Yes. Oh, God . . . great. . . . Everything's starting to spin."

She likes that. The man has a lot of romance in him. Awkward but genuine. That's something she can learn from him. She strokes him faster, watching his face tighten, the nervous grimaces, the heavy sighs. Struggling to come, to hold it off, to say something sweet.

"Don't think, Robie. . . . Just let it rip, sweetheart."

"Sweet . . . heart. Ohhhhhh. God. Oh, please, thank you." He's gasping, and trying to catch it all with the napkins, doubling over a little, smiling gratefully into her serene face. "Great," he tells her, "that was . . . wonderful."

She gives him some last squeezes, then puts it back in his pants, zips him up. "Oh, look." When she brings her hand up between them, there's a fleck of white on her first finger. Slowly she puts the hand close to her mouth and licks off the fleck. "Hhmmmm."

"Ohhhh," he says, staring blankly at her, "you'll make me hard again."

Kathy smiles. "Good. Now you go back and put out a great paper and think about me every second."

"Kiss me again," he begs. "You're just . . . so . . . wonderful."

"Twice in the same day," she smiles. "I must be doing something right."

"Kathy . . . everything."

Chapter 10

Robert wasn't so tentative. Now he moves on her heavily, urgently. More than he normally does. Anne tries not to think about this. To go with him, enjoy it. His hands grip her strongly. No, there's something different. And it's the opposite of what she was worrying about the last week or so. Thinking he might be distracted, losing interest, becoming bored.

How could this be? Suddenly it seems the most terrifying thing, that her husband should be *more* dramatic and passionate.

When she thinks this, she loses her sexual tension. Another kind pervades her. Intellectual tension, she thinks it might be called. A puzzle takes over her mind. Why would Robert change?

And she shamelessly channels this tension, this confusion and anger, into a small fake orgasm. Not so much to deceive

Robert, or flatter him. But to hide her thoughts. To give herself freedom to wrestle with the puzzle.

Robert finishes and slowly eases his large body off her much smaller one, curling up close to her in the dark. The way he normally does, one knee up on her thighs, one arm across her body. Whispering into her ear. "Good night, sweet Anne."

"That was nice, Robert. . . . 'Night."

She lies there, eyes wide open. How does a man become more passionate, suddenly? How? She feels so stupid, so ignorant. But she comes back again and again to where she started. Something has changed. She doesn't trust this change. Indeed, if she looks it full in the face, she's terrified.

Robert's already half asleep. She knows his breathing so well. He's sliding . . . slowly off. Stirring next to her. Tossing a little, the way he does. He'll finally roll away, once asleep, settle on his back, maybe keep one leg against her.

Suppose, she thinks, he is bored with me. Losing interest. . . . Oh, it's all my fault, I'm sure. But he feels guilty, I suppose. So he tries to hide it, tries not to hurt me. Overcompensating, the shrinks would say. I don't know. Everything between us is so comfortable, so unassuming. He could pull away and *that* would become part of our pattern. It'd be normal for us. He wouldn't have to feel guilty. Sincerity, that was always Robert's long suit. It's not like him to pretend things.

It's almost, she thinks, as if he doesn't *know*. Right, that's it. He's changed, in bed anyway, and he's not even aware of it.

Anne feels her body go rigid. This is the most frightening road to go down. For what could cause such a change? What? Or who?

She doesn't want to think about this. She *wants* to go to sleep. So she can juggle numbers all day. But she can't see any way around her deduction. Oh, it's too monstrous to think about. Monstrous and inconceivable. And yet what is happening everywhere you look? And who's always the *last* to know?

She feels the tension building in her body. She presses on her stomach. A knot has formed in the solar plexus. She kneads it with her fingers.

Oh, I'm overreacting. What's wrong with me? Wait until next time, see if it happens again. See if *what* happens? I've got a hot husband, who can't get enough of me? Ha! Can't accept a gift, can I? The glass always half empty. I hate that about myself. But what is going on? Seriously, even a klutz like me learns a few things. . . .

Dear God, all this because Robert really *went at it*, as they say. Maybe he stopped on the way home at a porno store, looked at some dirty pictures, got himself worked up. Well now. Maybe he's got some hidden around here.

Anne smiles in the dark. This is a nice theory. It has the virtue of having only two humans in it, plus porno. Robert and herself. Yes, she always saw it that way. Until they were gray and doddering and then in the ground, side by side. Their children coming now and then to put flowers on the graves.

She concentrates on this long life together, turns it around and around in her mind, finally drifts off in a restless sleep.

PART

Chapter 11

Robert arrives twenty minutes after Kathy, at five. A little hotel on East 32nd Street. Everything worked out. False names. No records. Never seen together. Kathy insists, says it's only smart. She calls in the reservation at lunch, says her husband is flying in later from Denver.

Robert comes up the elevator, marveling at the things he's doing, things he never imagined. Plotting and scheming. Lying, that's the bottom line. Lying all the time. To Anne. To his colleagues. To himself? That's where it gets tricky. Then when he imagines he's getting a clear fix on things, he thinks of Kathy's eager sexuality, of some extravagant little detail of her enthusiasm for him, of how pretty she is, how vital and alive. And he can't think. He can only want. And count the seconds until the next time he can look into those lovely eyes and touch her.

Coming out of the elevator, he can feel his heart, sense

the pulse of his blood. It's madness, he thinks. . . . What if Anne finds out? . . . Have to stop. Pull back. . . .

Instead he almost runs down the hall. Knocks three times and goes in the unlocked room. The light subdued. He has to strain to see. Bed, chairs . . .

"Hello?"

The room's L-shaped, with a little area to the right. He turns that way. Sees a wide cabinet. Kathy sitting on top, in the middle, naked, hips forward, her knees up and far apart.

"Hi, lover."

He feels faint from a rush of emotions. His first thought is to drop on his knees before her, in veneration, in hunger for her sweet body.

He lurches closer, puts a hand on her knee. Smiles down at her. Marveling at the shapeliness of her breasts. She reaches out to touch his balls. He almost leaves the floor, they're so on edge.

"Do what you want," she says. "Please. That's all I ask."

He kisses her hard. His fingers curl up inside her. So hot, so wet.

She's got his pants open, holding his prick. She falls slowly sideways, stretching out on the cabinet, pulling him along. He stares fascinated as she steers his prick toward her mouth.

He wants to do everything at once. Come. Kiss her. Tell her one compliment after another. Run screaming from the room. She's licking him. "Kathy . . . Kathy . . . wait a minute." I've never wanted a woman like I want you. He can't speak the words. But they're true.

She ignores his gibberings, his confusion, does what she wants with him.

He pushes away from her. Staring down, his face contorted. She smiles. Yes, lover?

"Let's start over," he says. "Sit just the way you were. . . . I have to see it again."

She pushes herself up, squares her knees, spreads her

thighs outward. Showing him the black hair, the intricate flesh. He undresses blindly, then drops to his knees. His hands touch the floor. He moves closer, closer. Smells her. Takes deep breaths of her. He licks her for a long time, slow and dreamy, then more roughly. She rubs his hair, whispers to him, "My man."

Finally he stands, pulling her up with him, settling her down on his prick. He turns toward the bed, topples over. Puts everything out of his mind, screws her as hard and fast as he can. Holding her ass, pounding away. Do what I want, she says . . . by God, this is what I want.

"Don't come," she says.

"What?"

"Just stand up, you know, on your knees." She pushes him. "Come in the air, I want to see it."

He straightens over her. Staring at her perfect body. Jerking himself off in a startling high arc, the come splattering on her breasts and stomach.

She dabs at it, smiling up at him. "Whoa, sweet baby. They felt *that* down on the street."

An hour later, they're dressing. Kathy walking around naked as long as possible, Robert notices. Or in her elegant underwear.

"Ohh!" she says. "I feel great. How about you?"

"Can't walk," he says. "Other than that, great."

"Hey, Robie," she says, standing close in front of him, "good sex is important. I happen to believe that. But I want you to know something. This is not all fun and games for me. You know that, don't you?"

"Yes . . . I do."

"I care a lot about you. No, I'll say it. I love you. Nice words."

He stares at her, his eyes bleary. "I can't stop thinking about you," he says factually.

"It's a start." She laughs. "I know, I know, the married guys never leave their wives." She rubs his chest, smiles sort of sadly. "That's all right. I'll take my chances. You're worth it. Personally, I think we're a perfect match."

He stares some more, amazed at how she touched the big question and just went past it. He embraces her almost feverishly, from desire and confusion and something else, gratitude perhaps. For what she's given him; and that she keeps on giving more.

She seems sometimes to think for him, which is frightening. But still a gift. Or they're so attuned that their thoughts arrive at the same point? Maybe, he thinks, that's what real love is. Oh, no question about it, he does love her.

The decision is like a canyon in front of his feet, but in that instant he sees himself somehow on the other side, leaving his wife behind. He and Kathy will always be together, locked in an endless embrace.

Kathy gives him a final kiss. "You go first," she says, "catch your train."

•••

Kathy takes a cab to a restaurant near Penn Station. To meet Louise again, quiet her down. Goddamned Keith.

Louise is waiting inside, smoking nervously.

"Alright, alright," Kathy says, "how bad is it? You're here, in one piece. Louise! You are sure he didn't follow you, right?"

Louise smirks. "I'm sure."

They hug, then Kathy says, "Relax. You're here to live it up." She tells the girl with the menus, "Looks like we need the smoking section."

They get a table by the far wall, nobody close. Fold their coats over nearby chairs. "This looks good, Louise. Now we can carry on."

They order martinis. Louise lights another cigarette. "Nice place," she says, glancing around at the black and chrome decor. She plays with the matches, rests her elbows on the black table. Sort of nervous, but giving Kathy this smug look. "Well, don't you look all rosy-cheeked? Been doing anything you wouldn't tell Mom about?"

Kathy laughs. "Alright, now tell me about Keith."

"Let's wait for the drinks. Look at men."

"You got it."

Kathy feels good, fairly calm. Nothing but time, now that Robie's on a train home. The martinis come and the women touch glasses. "To you," Kathy says.

"Thanks, I need it." Louise sips half her drink, goes back to puffing on the cigarette. She's always a little high-strung. Her face pretty enough but tense, watchful. Too much mascara. Always strutting her shoulders so nobody misses the boobs. Kathy never knows what she'll say next, or what mood she'll suddenly land in.

Louise sighs at length.

"Like I said, I have a long day. I'm beat to hell. Probably a good thing in the circumstances. I come home and there's your ex-man sitting on the sofa, watching the basketball game, having himself a beer. One of mine, I think. I do happen to have two locks on my door."

Kathy shakes her head. "Resourceful guy."

"Oh, yeah, Kath. Thank you for sharing that."

"He's just showing off."

"Yeah, he can get in my place any time he wants and kill me. He showed me that much."

"Louise, be calm, be serious. The man's probably on probation somewhere. He is not going to do anything that would hurt him. He's selfish like that."

"He pointed out he could rape me and beat me up a little and nobody would do a thing. He also said I'd like it."

Kathy laughs. "What a guy. . . . Sorry."

"You can laugh. I'm on the front line here."

"The guy's a dinosaur. Totally obsolete. And he doesn't know it. Gives him a certain power, I guess. Charm, too, I guess. Look, Louise, it doesn't do us any good to be upset. If he ups the ante, you'll tell him where I am. That's all. Then

I'll have to deal with him. Really. I appreciate you trying to keep him off."

"He wants you back, Kath. You get this or you don't?"

"Doesn't matter. Maybe he wants to own the New York Yankees. Same difference."

Louise makes her evil grin again. "He thinks you want him back. 'Don't let her kid you,' he tells me. 'Girl goes to sleep thinking about this,' he says, grabbing you know what."

"What, Louise . . . his Harley?"

"Yeah, right, Kathy."

"Give me a cigarette."

"Touch a nerve, sweetie?"

Kathy lights up, takes a deep drag, then mostly plays with the cigarette. "Jesus, Louise, you are something. You think I'd let a low-life like Keith threaten what I've got going?"

"And what is that, Kathy? I'd like to know."

"Don't be so tough. I hope you're not pissed because I'm trying to improve my life. Come on."

"I love you. No, I'm not pissed about that. But I'll tell you. My brother comes home and says he's born again, I'd want some *particulars*. Guy's almost as bad as Keith, so you understand my point."

"I don't like that, Louise. I'm not born again, okay? I moved to Manhattan, got a pretty good job, nice little apartment. Starting over, not born again."

"Now how'd this happen—exactly? You maybe fuck somebody?"

"Louise, stop. I went to the paper in Bergen, got a job as a secretary, office admin. Boring bullshit job. But I figured—pretend I'm an adult, give it a chance. Suddenly they need somebody to help with some promotions. Slogans. I was in some meetings, pitched in my bit. And they say, now you're doing it full time. Eight months later I see an ad for a job over here, doing the same stuff. I figure, let's take a shot. I walked in like I owned the place. Smiled a lot. Looked everyone in the eye. Whatever they asked, I said, 'No problem.' Truth. That's the way it's been. No problem."

Louise shrugs in surrender, maybe get Kathy back to what matters here. "I'm sorry. . . . Congratulations."

"I think I'm on a roll. I feel good. Hell, I feel great."

"Rolled right into Mr. Right?"

Kathy shrugs *yes.*

"Uh, tingling all over?"

"Louise. Maybe you had some bedside manner. *Once.*" They stare at each other, smiling. "Hey, you jealous?"

Louise shrugs. "I don't know. Maybe." Her expression softens. "Yeah, maybe. If it's real, what you got."

"Oh, it's real."

Louise smirks. "Oh, married guy?"

"Would you *stop?* I told you, he's not that married." She smiles. "Less all the time."

"Oh? He's leaving his wife for *you.*"

"Hell," Kathy says, "in his place, *I would.*"

"Got to give it to you. You got good attitude." She waits a few seconds, blows smoke up. "So you been fucking this guy. Like an hour ago. Which put the red in your cheeks."

Kathy thinking, Funny, a few years ago, I'd be telling her the size of the guy's dick. Now it seems wrong. I live in Bronxville. We may fuck, but we do not talk so much.

"That smile means what?" Louise peers hard at her.

"He's a fine man. Sorry, but I'm not telling you"—Kathy starts laughing—"how high he comes."

"What! Tell me. Seriously, you saw?"

"A joke. Louise. Listen to me. About Keith. The reason he can't find me is because I don't want to be found. I do not want to see him again, not ever. And I am not afraid of him. Are you getting this?"

"I think so."

"You think I'm telling the truth?"

"Yeah, I guess."

"Don't fucking guess, damn it. Believe it. Then convince him. Not such a big deal."

"Oh, yeah. . . . Suppose he shows up in your house? What do you do then?"

"Whatever it takes, Louise. Whatever it takes."

Louise sits back. "Really? Hmmmph. Maybe I am convinced."

"Bet your last dollar, bitch."

"Wow. . . . Bitch, is it? I guess you're buying."

"Louise . . . of course, I'm buying."

"This guy really a good lay? The married guy."

"He's a wonderful man, Louise. He also happens to be six-one, a hundred and eighty-five or so. One does so appreciate a big man, don't you find?"

Louise shakes her head. "Kathy . . . Kathy . . . Kathy."

Chapter 12

"Good, do it that way," Robert tells the reporter. "Done. Next."

He sits stiffly, trying not show how agitated he feels. Wearing a striped shirt, the tie knot loose. He's at the head of a large table, two reporters to his left, another two on his right. Only one woman. He's grateful he doesn't find her attractive. The state he's in, he might gawk at her.

"The aid package," one of them says. "Alright, the money comes through, we say PRESIDENT TRIES TO BUY VOTES. The money's not coming, we say UP YOURS, PRESIDENT TELLS BIG APPLE. Or words to that effect."

"Come on," the woman says, "the President can't win."

"Winning's not his job," Robert says, his voice quiet, carefully controlled. "His job's selling papers."

"Here, here."

"How about PRESIDENT'S AID PACKAGE SAVES DEMOCRATIC MACHINE?"

"Shit, that's almost the truth. You can't put stuff like that in the newspaper."

They all laugh. Energetic, restless, vaguely rumpled people. The kind of faces you see gambling in Atlantic City. Robert hopes they won't notice what has happened to him. No, they have to notice. He's coming apart in front of them, for Chrissake.

A reporter says, "I want to do something new on the drug wars."

"Who cares?"

"Right! They keep shooting kids, that's the only story. They just kill each other, hell, you're happy to hear—"

"The city ought to regulate these jerks. You know, make 'em take shooting lessons."

They're all laughing, arguing, interrupting each other. Robert likes it. People acting silly won't notice him.

"Look, the city regulates a business, they leave. Maybe it's an angle."

"A Department of Drug Dealers. Yeah, it'll work. A whole new bureaucracy for the mayor's cronies. And finally the dealers move to the Sun Belt. Let's put the paper behind it."

"Sweet. Genius."

"Hey, I got a serious idea. Why don't we offer rewards, you know, for the baddest guys? Like those Old West wanted posters. Say $10,000. Information leading to arrest and conviction."

"That's great. Better $25,000. Jesus, that'll get the community behind the cops."

"I see it. We call it Dealer Lotto. Here's the pitch. Don't waste your dollars on those bogus gambling schemes, better chance of getting hit by lightning, et cetera. The *New York News* offers a real payout. Just rat on some fuck who should be doing ten to twenty anyway. . . . What do you think? Sure, it's a promotional gimmick. But it'll spin off a huge amount of copy for us, too. Human interest. Real news. It's got everything."

"You're serious?" Robert says, happy to be doubting somebody else's sanity. Put the spotlight on this poor schmuck. Very gravely, Robert says again: "You're really serious?"

The guy looks around. "Yeah. What's wrong? Hey, $50,000 makes it guaranteed. Really. We'd get great press all over the country. Think about the photo op. The mayor giving some guy with a bag over his head a big check. Then we do follow-up, see if the guy *lives* to spend the money. Dealer Lotto, get it?"

A secretary Robert hardly knows comes in to relay a message to one of the reporters. She leans over to speak in the man's ear. Robert glances down her blouse, sees the swell of her breasts. Lovely. She stands and smiles pleasantly. At him? Yeah, she's saying, Use me, big guy. This is all yours. She turns to leave. A tight gray skirt. Robert studies the shadow marking the crack of her ass. Yeah, she wants him to follow her out into the hall, wrap her legs around him right there. His groin jumps. He sees himself springing out of the chair.

It's so real. *Too* real.

Robert drops his right hand, grips the front of the chair, hard. Steady, man. He feels like Dr. Strangelove, trying to hold his arm down. Or his dick. Or his life. His eyes jump to the ceiling and he shudders inwardly. Kathy! The woman's made me a maniac. Is this what sexual dementia is like? You want to hump everything.

All I do, I just call, leave a secret message. In an hour, maybe much sooner, we're on the 26th floor, she looks so beautiful, we're kissing, her hand's in my pants, we're doing *anything I can think of.* . . .

No, no, hold it. We're meeting at five. Got to hang on. No, what I have to do is call Anne, tell her I'll be on the later train. Oh, God, Anne. . . . What excuse do I make this time?

"Robert, hey. Robert. Boss!"

One of the reporters is staring at him. A strange look on his face. See, they can tell. Robert's sure he stinks of sex, like a man doused in some bad cologne.

Robert sighs as if he's been thinking over some deep problem of journalistic ethics. "Yeah, just running that around in my head. It's a stunt. But why not talk to the legal department. It's your idea, run with it."

They talk story ideas for another thirty minutes, then Robert walks back to his office. Feeling like this obscene pulsing thing, sure that people are staring at him. He wonders who he can ask about it. Notice any change? Horns? Goat's feet? A tail? Hair sprouting everywhere? Damnit, there are huge tits in front of my face. You must have noticed. Are you blind?

Robert can't remember anything like this. He's obsessed, filled toe to head with thoughts of sex, with thoughts of her.

He slumps behind his desk. Tries to hold his head up, look intelligent. Oh, sure. A hard-on with an IQ of ten or twelve.

Think about it. When I was a kid, say sixteen, was that like this? Yeah, horny, horny all the time. But it's in the body. You jerk off and then you forget about it for a while. This is different. This is in my head, I think. Like a fever, a disease. I want Kathy all the time. I want *something*. . . .

I've got to call Anne, tell her I'll be late.

He stares at the small color portrait of Anne on the right side of his desk and winces. She's so nice. So trusting. The most decent person. . . . She deserves better than this. It's just too nuts. It can't go on.

He studies her, the smart face, the soft smile. Why can't *they* have what . . . what he and Kathy have? It hurts to think about it. They're both waiting. Maybe that's it. For the other one to do something, to take the lead, be aggressive. Is that it? Robert isn't sure. They're too well bred? They're too timid? What the hell is it?

For a few minutes the lust fades away. A rush of guilt takes its place. He feels sad . . . he feels like a failure. He can't pick up the phone.

No, I'll call Kathy, meet her on 26, cancel, tell her it's no good. Got to cool this down.

I'll explain it to her. Kathy, you are wonderful. Maybe the most wonderful woman in the world. But I am married and we really ought to keep our balance.

He imagines what'll happen. She'll look at him with this slightly pitying expression. He knows he'll feel like a weakling.

She'll say what she said once before: "Maybe, Robie, I'm basically a more serious person than you are. Women usually are, don't you find? It's never just fucking for us."

He'll feel like a real jerk.

Then she'll smile and joke, "Of course, sex is nice, too. Stand closer and I'll tell you what I thought up. You will *love* this. . . ."

Then he'll feel like an engorged penis, six-feet, one-inch long.

He snatches up the phone.

Be a man, he thinks. It's the best sex imaginable. That's good. I *deserve* this. A gift from God. I love Kathy. I really do.

Damnit, man, call Anne, tell her you'll be late. Anne, Anne, Anne. . . . We have to talk. . . . I'll tell her the truth. Anne, this is bigger than I am. I can't say no to this. . . .

Or maybe I just jerk off in the bathroom, calm down, then I could talk to Kathy rationally. Kathy, please, let's be reasonable about this.

Maybe meet her on the street, so even if she gets to me, we can't do anything. Yeah, what about that?

Robert leans his elbows on desk, pressing his hands back through his long hair, rubbing his face. The skin feels hot.

Chapter 13

Anne comes back from a meeting with her immediate boss, a woman named Estelle. A woman who smiled and said, "Don't worry, dear, your future at this company is assured."

Translation: No promotion for you, drone, now get back to work. And why is there no promotion? Because, Anne guesses, Estelle wants a man in the slot. Oh, yes, *slot.* Good word.

Anne settles heavily at her desk, sighs, mutters, "Damn you, Estelle, I deserved that. . . . Oh, God, forgive me my trespasses as I forgive those . . ." She tries to go back to work.

Instead she stares at a large framed photo on a side cabinet. Her and Robert, two years ago. Look at him. Isn't he something? That big sincere face, the longish brown hair. A real man, or real enough for me, and yet a real person. They say women are slow to fall in love. Took me about two dates. And I thought, yes, if I can swing it, he's the one. Then you spend a year trying to let it happen. Pretending you're surprised by the discovery that *I love you.*

And now what have I done? Am I losing him? Could such a thing happen? She stares at herself in the photo. She hardly comes up to his chin. She appears, she thinks, serious . . . contained . . . quiet . . . intelligent. Yes, all that. But pretty or glamorous or sexy? She stares. Not sure. Uncertain. Or have I driven him away because I'm so dull? Oh, dear God. A tax specialist. Well, *what* could be more boring?

She thinks of him at the paper in Manhattan. A dynamic, exciting job with smart, offbeat people. The pulse of the city driving them all. She's seen it, seen him in action. And here I am in dreary little White Plains, sinking in spread sheets. Numbers, numbers, numbers. Many of which have hardly any connection with reality.

She laughs. *Whatever that is.*

She works in a slow, distracted way, suddenly realizing it's past twelve thirty and she hasn't accomplished very much. She decides she doesn't want company just now, that she'll go out for lunch alone. She walks three blocks to a small coffee shop, not the kind of place that lawyers are likely to go to. The streets are wet and chilly. Everything seems gray and sullen.

No, she decides, it's just me; the streets look just like they always look on a damp day in March.

She sits toward the back, orders the chicken-salad plate. A light lunch for a light appetite.

I mustn't be rash, she thinks. But I also don't want to be a fool. . . . Be a fool or look foolish? Interesting distinction. Well, I don't want either, now that I think about it, so the heck with that distinction.

It all seems very complicated. Life, living, going on. . . .

Well, there is one thing. . . . She can't imagine herself confronting Robert. *Asking* him straight out. Hey, what's going on? No, she cannot do this.

She imagines the scene, just a bit, and it immediately becomes impossible. Flying off the roof of the house is more probable.

If you ask, she thinks, everything could blow up in your face. Who knows what drastic action he might take? Or what hurt he might feel? A marriage could be wrecked, or at least poisoned. You could end up far worse than you started.

Or he looks you in the eye and lies. And then where are you? He'll be more on guard, more cunning. Life will be even tenser.

Maybe it's better to lie to *myself,* just seal off the door to this room. Is this what most wives do? I bet it is.

Well, could she hint at her suspicions? Even that is difficult to imagine. *Geee,* dear, is that lipstick on your collar? Oh, wine? Of course it is.

The thing is, she decides, I can't get ahead of myself. Here I am with my miserable little suspicions, my damaged little feelings. Thin air probably. My own fault, in any case. And what? I'm going to ruin a marriage with a single sentence? It's crazy even to think about it. I don't have any evidence at all. Not really.

Anne pays for the lunch and goes back out to the street. She has some time. She decides to walk a few blocks, clear her head. It's quite cold. Good, she thinks. I'll take physical pain any time.

Evidence—now there's a friendly word. Not exactly friendly. In fact, ominous. But I know the word; I've used it a thousand times. I'm comfortable with it. Either there's evidence, somewhere in the world, or there isn't. What could be simpler than that? Well, not simple. But fundamental. Yes or no, on or off. The reason the computers work, the basis of all intellectual progress. Either something is or it isn't.

She finds this litany reassuring. She walks along unseeing, repeating the phrases. Evidence. There is some or there isn't.

Evidence.

But how does she get this magical stuff? She's up here in

White Plains. They live in Bronxville. The evidence, if there is such a thing, is in Manhattan. Well, most likely.

Anne walks six blocks up Dumont, turns over to Sullivan and then starts back along Granby toward work.

She considers things she's seen or read about. . . . Looking through his suits. For what? A matchbook? Hah! The man's working in the city of Manhattan. He could have anything in his suits. He got good grades in college. What's he going to do, carry around some girl's name? Maybe a little note—I LOVE CINDY. Come on. Alright, what about his address book? His briefcase? His papers? Same difference. Robert's a careful, organized man. He's not going to keep the evidence handy, where any moron of a wife can find it.

Well, alright, I'll look!

She laughs bitterly. This is *being* a fool or *looking* like a fool? One? Both? In any case, something dreadful. Something sneaky and devious and underhanded. Oh, God, and what if I find this evidence I'm talking about? Then the nightmare begins, right?

The firm's building is up ahead. Modern, solid, huge, oddly comforting. Never mind. The last thing she wants at the moment is to go back to work.

Anne thinks of her house, going from room to room. Is there someplace where he might leave a trace? What about the cars? The yard? She goes back into the house. The phone? Well, she could glance at the bills, see if there are any unusual numbers. Then what? She's going to call the numbers, say hello, are you the floozie messing around with my husband? Not too likely. Besides, Robert calls everywhere on business. There could be a dozen numbers I don't know. And, let's see, 212 and 914, I think the phone company treats them as the same. The Manhattan numbers aren't even listed. Well, I don't think they are. . . .

Anne returns to the lobby, goes up in the elevator, not feeling any better, but not any worse either. Truth is, she realizes, I'm a lot more angry with my boss than I can bear to admit. Basically, it's probably sexual discrimination. But so what? I'm going to charge her before the state's human rights commission? Fat chance. I'm going to tell the CEO? Oh, sure. Goddamn you, Estelle, I deserved that job.

Alright, she thinks, getting back behind her desk, let's take it out on the numbers. . . . Crunch some numbers. . . . Drive a truck through this loophole here. . . .

A call comes from a lawyer on another floor. "Yes, sure," she says. "No, Bingham has the file. . . . Get back to me when you're ready. That one's going to court, I'm afraid. . . . Yeah, bye."

Anne hangs up, then stares at the phone. Imagine, he could actually call her from our house. Well, that's what I was thinking—without thinking how crummy it is.

From our house?

Anne laughs at herself, imagining some hysterical woman on a soap opera saying, "I can't believe they did it *in our bed!*"

Well, come on. It *is* crummy, isn't it?

She stares at the phone some more, remembers there is a way to check on this. Some of the firm's phones have recorders on them, voice activated. Just in case clients forget their instructions. Maybe her own phone is on the system. The bosses are vague, they want a little paranoia.

Maybe not cheap, Anne thinks, but doable. At the moment that's a big recommendation.

She shrugs, tries to put it out of her mind. No, she thinks, it's not a bad idea. It's eminently doable. I just have to do it.

•••

The next day Anne leaves work a little early and drives to Ardsley, a small community fifteen miles to the northwest. She found the name in the Yellow Pages, tried to think of anyone they know there, any connection at all. Nothing.

She parks two blocks from the store. Still thinking of turning back. Deciding instead she'll proceed as though it's no big deal, proceed until there's some real obstacle. *Then* she'll turn back, give up this foolishness. This—to be more honest—treachery.

She walks by the small shop twice, checking out the small commercial street, the feeling it gives her. There isn't one, she decides. Just a store called Sensible Security. Just a potential customer coming to ask a few questions.

The man behind the counter is old enough to have some white in his thick hair. He's heavyish, with slow, thoughtful movements. He glances at her with a polite, concerned expression. All of this Anne finds reassuring. There's really no reason to turn back.

Anne explains what she might need, in general terms. The man looks at her with the blandest expression imaginable. She realizes that people must come in all the time with bizarre personal problems, problems they lie about outrageously. Still, he doesn't seem suspicious or critical. He listens, he answers.

In the store hardly five minutes, Anne decides that this is the man. She has the sense of falling. . . .

"Alright, then," she says, "let's be more specific. No one must know about this but you and me. Ever. No third person whatever. Is this possible?"

"I can promise that."

"Oh, if someone walks in the door now, I'm going to walk to the back. You would understand?"

"Of course."

"I would pay you in cash. There would be no bill, no other record. . . . Well?"

"Well, I'll record the cash sale. However, I can somewhat miswrite the name and address. Or you can make up a business name. No law against that."

"Now, I would contact you. You would never contact me. I think that's important."

"Of course."

"You would come to the address and personally install the machine. Correct?"

"Yes, as agreed." A little smile.

"You have a vehicle . . . how would it be marked?"

"I have a car, unmarked. Or I could come by taxi."

Anne thinks about her street, wondering who might notice this arrival, what chance occurrence could lead to somebody asking Robert about the strange car in the drive.

The street curves somewhat, so that only a few houses on the other side have a good view of her house's front. One couple she doesn't know. A second couple works, and so does a third. Well, it's probably better to do it publicly, in a routine way. A car stops for ten minutes, delivers something, who would notice.

"How long will the installation take?" she asks.

"If you are sure the wiring is in the basement, not much time at all. I suggest that you check the situation carefully, looking at things from my point of view. Basically, you just clip it on. And hide it. The model I recommend is all solid state. Quite compact."

"How long would I need to learn to operate it?"

"I'll show you now."

"No, I'll need to think about all this. Your background is what? Police? Electronics?"

"The latter, actually, by way of teaching high school science."

Anne smiles. "How charming." Teaching, she thinks, yes, that's probably what I should be doing. "Well, Mr. Martin, thank you. I'll be in touch."

"When you are ready," he says.

"Thank you," she says again, trying to mimic his detached manner. But inside she feels quite giddy.

Chapter

14

Kathy's sitting on top of him, still wearing blue panties, her breasts hanging close to his face. She smiles down at him, with that smile of hers. Sometimes it seems only playful, as if they're teenagers at a beach party. Sometimes mischievous, telling him it's really not that bad, anyway not final. Sometimes, as now, evil. As if she knows three times what he knows about life, and one of the things she knows is that they have gone over the edge and he's never coming back. Practically speaking, Anne's . . . already a *widow.* Oh, God.

Kathy holds his face between her hands and leans over to kiss him, sticking her tongue straight down into his mouth. Then she smiles very close to his face. "Robie, sweet Robie," she says.

He feels breathless, unable to speak, not just from the physical effect she has on him. But also from the confusion in his mind, the way his moods jump. He fumbles with her heavy breasts, finding the nipples. Everything he does feeling evil, wonderfully evil.

I deserve this, he tells himself. It's the best, it's everything a man dreams of, and I've got it.

She pushes two fingers into his mouth, and he sucks on them. With her other hand she strokes his chest.

She moves her ass around on his hard prick. Then she raises up, slowly, smiling at him, and very delicately pushes the blue fabric aside, and aims his prick up into her. He watches it disappear into the black hair as she settles down on him.

"Uummmmmm," she says. "I've got you now."

"Oh, yes," he says, with a strained voice.

"I'm doing the fucking now," she says.

He nods, okay, okay.

Kathy straightens her back, arches slightly away from him. She seems very tall now. She rises and falls on him, going right to the top of his prick, wriggling on it, making him think it's slipping out. But she keeps it in her and then drops forcefully down on him.

"Don't come, Robie," she whispers down to him. "I want to fuck you for a long, long time. I can't get enough of you."

That almost finishes him right there. He gasps, tries to think of something else. The walls of this motel. What the ceiling is made of . . . some kind of sound-proofing material, isn't it? Some faint voices coming from the TV. . . .

Then she falls over on him, puts her face on his. "Just kidding, lover. Don't you know that?" The big smile. "You come any time you want. With us, there aren't any rules. You *know* that."

Suddenly she stands up on the bed. Staring down at him for a moment. Then she steps off the bed and walks across the room. She leans against the wall and says, "See?"

"Oh, geez," he mutters. "Kathy . . . come back."

"I've got to pee." She pushes her panties down to the

floor, then starts toward the bathroom. "Come on in here, I'll show you something."

•••

They're dressed, it's almost time to go. Robert can hardly speak. They're sitting on the edge of the bed, side by side. He puts his right arm around her neck, lets his hand hang by her breast. Even exhausted, he thinks about taking her clothes off, starting over. It's crazy, he thinks, but it's a fact. Never mind, this is as calm as I get. I'm doing it. . . .

"It's the right thing," he says weakly. "We should get married." There, the words are out.

"Robie, you're proposing!"

"Yes, Kathy. I'm asking . . . please marry me."

"Hey, you! On the floor." She smiles.

He grimaces as he spins down on one knee before her. "You're right." He puts his left hand on her thigh. The other hand finds a small box in his jacket pocket. "Kathy, please marry me . . . as soon . . . when we can."

She watches him with a sweet and amused smile. Boy, he does struggle, doesn't he? Took his time, too, like there was some doubt or something. Alright, it's been tough for him—all I have to do is watch him to know that. And now here he is, on one knee, asking to make me Mrs. Kathy Saunders. Well, I think I might consider it. . . .

"I'd be honored," she says, more gravely, taking the small box.

"It's not an engagement ring, Kathy. Uh, you couldn't wear that yet. . . . It's just a present."

Kathy opens the Tiffany box and finds a slim gold bracelet. She smiles at him. "It's a *big* wedding ring, isn't it?"

He nods.

"It's sweet. And it's smart. Just what I expect from my man. I am so happy."

She puts the bracelet on and then hugs him. Leaning into

him, knocking him backward. He smells her perfume and feels her breasts on his face and, as they topple over, her soft weight on his chest. It's right, he thinks. I'm glad I did it.

"Yes, yes, yes," she says into his eyes. "Yes."

"Thank you," he says earnestly. "For everything."

"We belong together, sweet baby. All our lives were working toward this point."

"That's a nice way to think about it."

"It's the way I *always* thought about it."

He stares, amazed again by her confidence.

Chapter 15

The man next to Robert says, "Well, you can see why the guy was great with women."

That catches Robert's attention. "Yeah, why?"

"He looks in their eyes and says what they want to hear. He campaigned the same way and now he's running the country like that. Of course, we don't use the word liar."

Yeah, well, that's not me . . . is it? Robert stares at the grim landscape of the Bronx. His train's about fifteen minutes from Grand Central. He fidgets, says uneasily, "I see what you mean."

Another day of fires and murders, corruption and urban collapse, coming up. Another day of being in the same building with Kathy. Another day of deciding that this is the day—he'll get his thoughts together, go home and tell Anne the truth. Calmly and honorably. And she'll understand. And, well then, they'll get divorced.

"You vote for him," the man wants to know.

"Yeah, I did."

"Glad?"

"It was a tough election. To choose, I mean."

"That's the truth. You think the guy's maybe a little off? There's something . . . that W. C. Fields look. . . ." The man shrugs, sees Robert staring out the window, does the same. "Jesus, look at this . . . wasteland."

Robert nods. Yeah, this is the day, he decides. I'm going to do it tonight. It's inevitable anyway and, uh, I know it's right. And given what's going on, it's the only fair thing to do. I mean, come on, the dishonesty is what upsets me. The deception. The . . . hypocrisy? No, that's not it. It's not a moral matter, not for me. It's between me and Anne. We've always told each other the truth. We have to keep doing that. She expects it. She wants it. It's a personal matter. I owe her this. And she owes me her understanding. She'll give me that. Nobody asks for something like this to happen. Well, I didn't. I didn't go looking. It found me. Really, you can walk down the street and a safe falls on you. Or you see something in the gutter, and it's a winning lottery ticket. There it is, you have to pick it up. You don't, you're a fool. I mean, I'm not sure about God running around giving people gifts. But this is as close to that as it gets. A higher love.

Kathy is just extraordinary. I think about her, I get goose bumps, or a hard-on. Something, *bang*, visceral, right from the center. But sex and all that aside, Kathy is really an exceptional person. Well, so is Anne. But you take all the qualities together, Kathy is amazing. And she's not complacent, not sitting on a pat hand. I really like that. The feeling I get, I've got to keep chugging if I want to keep up. "VP Marketing," she says. "Five years. Count on it." Wow. . . .

"What do you do?" the man asks.

"Editor at *New York News*."

"Live in Westchester?"

"Yes."

The man smirks. "They should make all you people live in Manhattan. Damned limousine liberals are killing the place. Pushing all the bullshit for everybody else to live with, then they go back to Scarsdale."

Roberts stares at him. "My wife works in White Plains. It was sort of a compromise."

"Ummmm?"

"Hey, I'd like to live in Manhattan." Robert smiles. "Maybe I will be. Besides, I'm not a limousine liberal. I report the news as straight as I can. It's an honorable profession."

"Yeah? Well, alright. You sound pretty serious about it."

"Yeah," Robert snaps. "I'm serious." He almost adds, Now leave me alone, go bother someone else, you pompous jerk. I'm serious, alright. . . . Seriously over my head . . . seriously ready to tell Anne . . . seriously hooked, *line and sinker.*

The train's in the tunnel under Park Avenue. People standing up to put on their coats.

Robert thinks about Anne and how comfortable they've always been with each other. Yes, that's it. Comfortable. We're best friends. That's what's going to make this work. We've always wanted what's best for the other. I'll explain to her, this is just something I have to do. You wouldn't want to stop me, would you, Anne? No, of course not. I'd do the same for you. . . . Well, alright, I'd have to. That's the point. If someone you love sees a way to achieve some kind of greater happiness, you have to wish them well. You have to *push them* onward.

Robert stands up and moves into the aisle. Feeling calm and resolute. It won't be so bad. It has to be done. My future is with Kathy. Anne'll see that right away. God, I'll always love Anne. I'd help her any way I could. The rest of our lives, we'll be friends. That's the way I want it.

•••

Robert gets off the train in Bronxville that evening with all the phrases worked out in his head. He wants to be ready for anything Anne might say, any objections. Well, there's really only one, that he's known Kathy only a few months. Seems like a much bigger part of his life than that. Everything's been so intense. A lot of anxiety about each step in the relationship. But, really, didn't he know almost from the beginning? She got inside his head right off the starting block. He worries about telling Anne precisely that. No point in hurting her feelings. Still, she may ask, how can you be sure?

He walks to his car, pushing the pieces of the scene around in his head. Really, the only thing he's concerned about is keeping the whole thing calm, logical, friendly. He doesn't want any crying, or anger, or hysterics. He might lose his composure, too. And then who knows what either one of them might say. No, the main thing is to be low key.

He drives the few miles to their house in a fairly good mood. Remembering what Kathy told him: "You'll do fine, lover." That way she talks to him sometimes. As though he's the student, and she's the teacher or the coach.

All through dinner Robert is on the edge of saying, "By the way . . ."

He stands an inch away from doing it. The silence of the house seems to have gotten louder. Well, that's it, no children. God, that's luck, he thinks, given what is happening now.

He's got the smell of the other woman on him. A fact that seems to seal the matter for him. Yes, this is the night. All the same, he feels somehow vulnerable, exposed by this fact. Something that must be kept secret, and this, he senses, gives Anne a small bit of moral superiority.

He watches Anne, thinking about their years together. They talk of almost nothing. Was it always like this? The silence seems louder.

In the kitchen, as they wash and dry the dishes, Robert inhales at length and says, "Oh, Anne, I've been meaning . . ."

He's wiping a plate as he turns casually to face her.

She looks back at him. Somehow very poised and still. Why is this surprising? Somehow very . . . steely.

"Yes, Robert?"

". . . to talk to you. . . ."

And he has a horrible vision that Anne will not be friendly and agreeable. That's odd. She's *always* been friendly and agreeable. All the same, he *feels* this strongly. She'll object and resist. She'll—oh, God—fight back. And what does that mean, concretely? He sees it with great clarity. It means a messy, painful, and very expensive divorce. No, this isn't what he had in mind at all.

"Yes?"

Robert fumbles with the plate, lets it roll out of his hands onto the sink. It bounces and spins, clattering for several seconds.

"Damn," he says. "Slippery little bugger." He fakes a laugh.

"It's all right," Anne observes mildly. "Now, you've been meaning . . . ?"

"Oh, what?" He acts puzzled. Shakes his head, looking around the room as if trying to remember something. "Went right out the window," he laughs.

She waits. Very poised, it seems to Robert. Well, really.

"Oh," he says. "Maybe it's that promotion you've been upset about. I just wish you wouldn't let it get you down." He smiles at her. "Maybe it's a lucky break, you know, in disguise. Do you really want a lot more responsibility?"

She shrugs, seeming to consider the question carefully.

"I mean," he hastens on, "don't you have more time the way things are now? In case, well," he almost says *we have children*, "you want to travel . . . or whatever."

She stares carefully at him. "Well, maybe you're right."

He wipes some dishes, thinking, God, who knows what she'll do? I mean, once she knows, there's no turning back, no putting things in a different light. Hello, I'm in love, I want out—that's a lot for her to deal with. She might get crazy on me. . . .

"Yes," Robert says after a moment, "it probably is a blessing, you know, in disguise."

Chapter 16

Anne sits at her desk in the second-floor den, looking over the bank statement, balancing their checkbooks, hers and Robert's. "Anne," he told her the first year they were married, "if my checkbook's only ten or twenty dollars off, that's good enough for me." She smiles, still not able to believe anybody could mean that.

At work, she has to make hundred-million-dollar budgets work out to the penny. If her own finances weren't handled the same way, she'd feel indecent, like going to the office without her clothes on.

Anne glances at her watch, thinks about her plan to leave Robert alone in the house. "Yes," she says softly, "I'm doing it." Alone for two hours, all by himself, nothing but Robert and a lot of phones.

She imagines the dark technology hidden in her basement. Waiting there for . . . what?

For Robert to call . . . whom?

Anne finishes with the checkbooks, then goes downstairs to the kitchen. She stares out the window into the backyard, sees Robert stretched out on one of the lounge chairs, reading the *Times.* Sections of the huge Sunday edition scattered on the grass.

Very bright out there. Definitely a spring day. Well, about time. But it must be still chilly. Robert's wearing a burgundy windbreaker.

She goes to the front closet to find a light coat, then out to talk to Robert.

"Anything I have to read?"

She stands near the foot of the chair, her arms crossed over her chest.

"The chess column," he jokes. "You can kind of skim over the rest. One of these days they'll be competition. . . ." He grins handsomely. Or is it tensely? "But not yet."

"Of course not," she says loyally. She walks over to look at the flower beds. "Things'll be coming up in a few weeks!"

"They better."

"Well," she says, "I have a little shopping to do."

He stares at her, eyebrows up. "Need any help?" Wanting to say—half a second from saying—*Anne, we have to talk.*

"Oh, no," she tells him, "you stay here. Rest up for tennis."

"Wilsons at four, right?" He can't say it. Damn, why is it so damned hard to do?

"Yes."

"I'll come along if you want."

"No, no. I have to see somebody about slipcovers. Boring." Like me.

"Alright," he says, settling back. Is he relieved? She's not sure. Maybe.

"I'll be back by, let's see, three thirty," she says as she turns toward the house. "Don't worry," she adds. "I won't be late."

Anne goes through the house toward the car. The good

wife on the way to do errands. She smiles faintly, bitterly. What errands? Call it what it is, she thinks. I'm setting a trap.

Anne gets in the car, shivering a little. At what she's become. Disloyal? Oh, yes. And scheming? That, too. And wasteful? The damned thing cost $368.

And why? There's still no evidence. No real evidence.

She drives the Volvo toward a friend's house. Stop there, kill time. Oh, Sally would be so shocked if she knew about that little box beneath the kitchen floor. Well, who wouldn't be shocked? Everybody I know would turn pale, and then probably disown me.

Or would they all say, "Well, of course, dear. We know all about Robert. We tried to tell you. . . ."

No evidence at all. And yet everything feels different. Is this because I'm thinking horrid, unthinkable thoughts? And I've somehow settled down to their morally debased level. Or is it simply that my instincts are right? And I am now, already, a woman who *used to* have a loving husband?

Anne pounds the steering wheel with her left hand. She can't remember feeling this sort of frustration.

"It's intellectual," she says aloud, waiting for a light. "You know two things. But you don't know three others. And you might never. . . . But, but they *are* knowable. Heck, Robert knows all of them. So the answers are all around me. . . . And I just can't quite reach them. . . ."

She thinks of the way he followed her into the shower that morning. "Oh, you look good," he said. And he kissed her and hugged her, and finally he got behind her and, well, it was very nice. Well, what is this? A lusty, attentive husband. And I can't enjoy it for what it might very well be. And why? She thinks over the details. Robert has followed her into the shower before. He's made love to her almost that same way.

But it wasn't the same. That's just it.

He didn't hesitate. He didn't ask. He didn't—what?—test the waters. That's the way he would do it before. He'd feel out the situation, circle around me a little. Wait for me to respond, to indicate one way or another, Sure, Robert, we can do it.

Ah, the Bold New Robert. That's just what is terrifying me. Something *has* changed. Robert has changed.

She waits too long to make a left turn, then accelerates in front of an oncoming truck. She hears a horn and brakes in the same instant. She sees the shadow of the truck rush by behind her right shoulder. She tenses . . . but there's no crash. She got away with it. She presses on the gas, keeps going. Too embarrassing to deal with. She's not paying attention, and she almost got killed.

"Anne! Please!" she scolds herself.

She sees a supermarket ahead on the right and turns into the big parking lot. Just sit perfectly still and say a little prayer, she thinks. Don't drive for ten minutes. Try to think clearly, for a change.

And the way Robert started to say something the other night, then he didn't. It just isn't like him. He's good with words, they're his business. He speaks in sentences and paragraphs. My husband does not say, "I've been meaning to mention something," and then forget what it is. Maybe in thirty years. Not now!

So what happened there? I remember, I heard a tone in his voice. I was alert, ready. But I was being very careful—I remember this clearly—not to react prematurely. Not to anticipate. Way back in my head I thought, Well, maybe he'll mention another woman. Then, a second later, I thought he could mention some pretext, a trip or something. Yes, I would have been very suspicious of a trip.

But mainly I was trying to be very neutral. Just washing the dishes. Just chatting. An ordinary wife who has no suspicions about anything whatever. I'm sure that's how I acted. There was no reason for him to stop like that.

So what happened?

Do I look different? Am I different? Is it me who's changing? Not Robert?

She leans forward until her forehead is on the hard steering wheel. Her eyes close.

So, she demands, how *should* I feel? What should I do?

Why can't I just be grateful? Good husband. Good sex. Good times. Oh, yes.

But suppose there is someone else. And he comes home each night and lies down beside me. It just makes me so angry . . . I can't think clearly.

She cries a little, feeling sorry for herself. Wallowing in the dreadful truth. She's not very interesting. Not nearly pretty enough. She got lucky, marrying Robert. But she overshot. What else could she expect? Finally, he drifts away.

She wipes her eyes, imagines the complicated little box waiting for Robert to call. The man said, "It's state of the art. Great little gizmo."

Anne smiles thinking of that phrase. Well, it's action. She's sure of that much. Doing something feels good. It was funny—she simply couldn't think of anything *else* to do.

She looks at her watch. Wonders if Robert is lying in the yard, thinking to himself, *Hell, Anne's out of the way. I could call her now.*

She glances around the parking lot, turns the ignition key, says, "Go for it, Robert."

Chapter 17

Robert's at his desk at the newspaper, sipping the morning cup of coffee, trying to think clearly, which seems to be harder and harder to do. Let's see, meetings at ten and eleven. Kathy appears in his head and she's undressing, more real than the room he's in. . . .

No, block that! Think about the garbage strike, the tourist who got killed two blocks away, anything. . . . Then Anne's there in his head and he sees them yelling, he sees her throwing things. Damn, no, please stop that! . . . There's got to be a better way. . . . Alright, what if I put it all down in a letter, get everything said before she can interrupt me. Right! I try to talk to her, she'll just go to pieces on me and we'll never get through it. . . . Never, never, never.

Robert's frowning thoughtfully as he finishes the coffee, puts the cup down. He glances over at the old IBM Selectric he keeps in the corner of his office, moves his chair toward it. Yeah, all the word processors are connected, maybe some jerk supervisor is checking everybody's work habits, personal memos. Jesus, the nerve of these people. . . .

He puts a piece of paper into the typewriter, starts typing.

My dear Anne,

The most amazing thing has happened. Amazing but also sad! You and I have been truly blessed.

Jesus, right, pile it on. . . . Yeah, this is good. I can hand it to her, some place public. Hell, I can messenger it to her at work. Then it's done. Let's see. . . .

We've had a wonderful marriage. I believe few men are as fortunate as I've been.

He sits back, reading the words over several times. Yeah, be gentle, be nice. Infinitely nice. Right! Lay it out like a lawyer—but poetically. So there's only one conclusion she can come to. Yes, Robert, you are right, she'll say. Go in peace. God bless you. Thanks, Anne, you're wonderful. Yeah, it'll be like A + B = C. This is what I should have done at the start. Jesus, can you imagine! You try to talk about something like this, everything's out of control before you know it, and you've got nothing but scars all around.

Robert goes on typing, watching the door now and then. Somebody's always stopping by. . . . Why're you using the typewriter, Mr. Saunders? . . . I guess I'm just an old-fashioned kind of guy, buddy. I think best on this old thing, can you believe it? . . . No, Mr. Saunders, I can't. . . . Well, buddy, fuck you.

Robert's smiling as he gets up and goes to shut his door. Yeah, let's concentrate, do this thing right. He sees Anne reading the letter calmly, nodding sadly but resignedly, *going with it.*

Then he's telling Kathy, everything's set, no problem, I told you I'd take care of it. What do I take off first, she wants to know. Wait a minute, wait a minute. This is important.

Robert sits down again at the typewriter, reads what he's got so far.

Chapter 18

Robie lies on his back, flopping his penis side to side. He stares across the room at Kathy's lean, well-proportioned body, the black bush she says she trims.

She's by the dresser, pouring champagne. She glances back, sees what Robie is doing to his penis. "Hey," she says, "stop that." She tosses her shoulders. "That's my job."

She comes back with the glasses of champagne, some croissants and Swiss milk chocolate. "All the things you love to eat," she says, sitting on the bed by his hip, her knees spread apart. Robie glances between her legs.

"Go ahead," she says. "I want you to memorize me. No matter what you're doing, you'll see my pussy in your mind."

"It's about that bad."

"Bad, hell. That's great." She leans way over and sloppy-kisses him. "You couldn't say anything sweeter to this girl. Except maybe, 'I do.' " She dribbles some champagne on his almost hairless chest, leans over again to lick it off him.

Robie's face tenses. "You know I'm not happy about it."

"Lover! Don't worry. Things are going fine. We're getting married. I want it. You want it. It'll happen."

Robie sees his wife's expression, in the kitchen, when he tried to mention the word divorce. Damn it. He thinks about the letter he's been carrying around all week—it just never seems to be the right moment.

"It's just so clear to me," he says, "no matter how I handle this, there's going to be trouble. Maybe she goes ballistic, starts yelling, calling a lawyer, ordering me out. I don't know. . . ."

"Robie." Kathy's voice is a little impatient. "She's your wife. You know best how to talk to her. It just seems to me you have to do it in a firm, decisive way. Then she sees it's more or less settled. A done deal."

Kathy plays with his penis, curls her fingers through the brown hair there. With her other hand she's holding a glass of champagne up close to her face, sipping now and then.

Robie watches her with fascination. She always seems completely given over to him and sex. As if all she can think of is getting him hard again and stuck in one opening or another. Then she surprised him a week back, telling him, "It doesn't make any difference if you get hard, Robie. Nice but not the main thing. You don't want to do anything, I'll lie here and look at your face and jerk off all by myself. I love looking at your face."

He thinks about her devotion, and regrets again that he disappointed her. He disappointed himself. He gets pissed every time he thinks about it. Damn Anne. He hates the thought that Kathy might think, well, that he's not in love enough, or not strong enough.

"Come down here and kiss me," he says.

When their faces are inches apart, he says, "I do love you. And I like you. And I lust after you. All three, probably more than any other time, any other woman."

"Probably?" Kathy laughs. "Who's the bitch? I'll kill her."

"No," Robie says earnestly, "you're in a class by yourself."

"Oh, I think I'll jerk me off right now. You mind?"

Robie stares.

"Only kidding, lover. I just wanted you to know you got the juices flowing. Thanks, big precious." She laughs in a girlish way. "I think I'll sit on your chest. So you can see how hot you make me."

The things she says! Robie feels his penis stiffen. She doesn't notice, swinging one knee over him, settling her weight on him, smiling down between her swinging breasts. "Now," she says, "tell me what you're thinking about. . . . Is it the economic condition of the country? . . . *No?* Is it the riots in Brooklyn? . . . *No?* By the way, what you're feeling . . ."

"What?"

"It's a special medical condition. It's called VFS. Vaginal fire syndrome."

She sort of smiles at him, waiting for Mr. Literal to catch up, join the party.

Robie finally laughs. "Oh. Haha. Yeah."

He thinks about Anne's expression, that time in the kitchen. He wonders why he assumed that of all the things she could do, she'd react just the way he wanted. Go, Robert, you're free to do as you please. *Of course* she'll make problems, maybe big problems. How can he chance it? Damn you, Anne! Be reasonable. Get out of the way.

Kathy studies him. "You're with me. You don't *think* about her. That's an order." She reaches behind herself to squeeze his penis, wake him up. "Oh," she's says, "it's alive. Well, half alive. That's *still* an order."

"The thing you have to remember about her," Robie says, looking away, wanting somehow to explain himself, "is that she spends her days telling big corporations how to save big bucks. Maybe they think of her as a tough cookie. She doesn't usually bring that side of her home. Wait . . . don't do that." He holds Kathy's arms. "One more minute. All I can tell you is that there was an instant when I saw it." He fumbles on, trying to find something good in his failure. "Maybe a couple instants. Thing is, this might be a blessing. I mean, once the cat's out of the bag, hell, I lose control. I think. Now we can look the terrain over. Move in just the right way. You know, while we still have the element of surprise."

Kathy listens for some sense in all this, not sure there is any. "Look, lover. The best thing for everybody is she disappears off the face of the planet. But that's not going to happen. So what are you going to do? You think of the story that will upset her the least. I'm repeating myself, right? But I'm a woman. This is what I'd want to hear, if you have to hear this kind of shit. It's not her. You still love her. But you've grown in a different direction. You need time and space. It happens a thousand times a day, you know."

Kathy draws her knees up, rests her chin on them. Staring almost straight down at him. Robie nods that he understands.

"You're sure she doesn't know, right?" Kathy asks.

"No, I know her. She'd ask me straight out. Or she'd be pissed all the time."

"How can you be so sure?"

"Well, you're married eight, nine years, there's patterns. You stay right in them, no problem. And my wife's emotional." Maybe too emotional, he thinks. "If there's a problem, she's going to . . . complain." He almost says *whine*, to make the point, but decides it's disloyal.

Robie glances down along her thighs at the glistening hair. He raises his hands to rub her back.

Kathy laughs. "I knew this weird guy believed in UFOs, abductions, all that alien stuff. So put her up on the roof at night. Maybe some green guys will take her away."

"That's not . . . very nice."

"Oh, Robie." Kathy giggles. "She might like it—sex with green men? Don't be jealous, now."

"I think now," he says, "I'm only jealous of you."

"You'll never have any reason to be jealous of me. . . . Hey, remember, I'm the one who should be jealous. I'm still the other woman."

"No. Not for long. I promise."

"Thanks, lover."

"This back-and-forth life is tough on me, you know. I want to be with you." Robie thinks how simple life would be if Anne got on a plane, and it crashed. . . .

"It was always fate, Robie. We belong together. You think God makes marriages?"

"Maybe."

"If He does, He made ours."

"Right."

"Now let me ask you an important philosophical question. You want to eat me? Or vice versa?"

Chapter 19

Kathy gets the call from Louise. The one she always half expected. Keith put the pressure on, slapped Louise around some. She told him what he wanted to know.

Alright, deal with it, Kathy tells herself. The hell with Keith. Let's do it.

She takes a personal day and goes to Hoboken. Visit the sick girl, least she can do. Crazy Keith probably waiting for her. What difference does it make? He knows where she works now. He'll show up sooner or later.

Outside the PATH station, Kathy finds a cab, tells the driver Louise's address and that she wants to cruise the street, make sure a certain someone is not around. Driver nods. What's he care? More money on the meter. Kathy sits in the left corner, checks in her purse for the little cylinder of Mace. She puts it in her right-hand coat pocket, the cap loose.

Louise lives on a block of six-story buildings, sort of run-down residential. No big Harleys in sight. Kathy gets out two blocks away and calls Louise from a pay phone, says she'll buzz three times, be waiting.

She puts a scarf over her hair, turns up the collar of her coat. Waits for some people going in the same direction.

"Hi," she says. "I might move in around here. What's the neighborhood like?"

"Oh, good," one of the women says. They're older; one's probably a grandmother, at least.

Kathy walks close to them, scanning the street, keeping the conversation going until she reaches Louise's building. "Wait a sec, will you?"

Kathy steps into the vestibule, buzzes Louise. When the door clicks, Kathy waves. "Oh, good, my friend's home. See ya!"

She's watchful going up in the elevator to the third floor, and stepping into the hallway. Louise opens the door at the end, calls out, "You're home."

Kathy walks in slowly, studying Louise. Three dark bruises on her face, maybe some she can't see.

Kathy holds her friend's shoulders. "I'm really sorry."

Louise shrugs. "I'm okay. I could've worked. But who wants all the questions."

"Well, you did everything you could for me. More. I'll always be grateful."

"Alright, alright, let's not get all serious. I'm watching Oprah, about lesbians who marry fags. Is this an exciting world, or what?"

"It's an exciting world."

Louise is wearing jeans and a turtleneck jersey. Very tight. "Hey, you got other injuries?" Kathy gestures at the jersey. "Or are you just trying to show off your tits?"

Louise makes a thin smile. "Still pretty good, huh?"

"You want to answer the question? You want to give a lady a drink?"

"Sorry. Make yourself at home. We'll get something, then sit over there in the IC unit."

Louise laughs as she goes to the kitchen, gets two glasses, a bucket of ice, a bottle of gin and a bottle of cranberry juice. "Buffet style," she says. "The way you like it."

Kathy takes her coat off, turns the TV off, sits on the living room sofa. A small one-bedroom apartment. Sort of undecorated-looking, as though Louise just moved in. Kathy thinks she's been here two years.

After they mix up some red gin, Kathy says, "So what, really, is the damage?"

"Just what you see." Louise is in the big easy chair, legs folded beneath her. Her light brown hair combed out almost straight. No makeup. She makes Kathy think *sexy librarian.* "And he grabbed my arms real hard. They're blue. Shook me a lot. I think he likes that."

"Makes your tits jump."

"He said that."

Kathy waits. "And?"

"Well, he was real dramatic. Scared me more than he hurt me."

"That's Keith. Guy ought to go to Hollywood. Get paid for acting all the time."

Louise laughs.

"I notice you're not all that angry, Louise. You're nuts, you know, if you even think about this guy for one second."

"I know. I know." She glances around vaguely. "Look, the main thing is you. He said he'll be seeing you." Louise watches for her reaction.

Kathy sighs wearily. "It doesn't matter, Louise. It just doesn't matter."

"Nothing's left? No sparks?"

"Nothing. Everything he stands for, I've moved past it. You like Keith. You take him."

"Maybe I would . . . but he likes you."

"He doesn't like me. He wants me."

"Well, that's a compliment, isn't it?"

"Oh, sure. Louise, he wants me on the back of his Harley. Prize pussy. Jerking him off on the New Jersey Turnpike while we're doing eighty."

"Damn. Thinks big, doesn't he?"

They both laugh together, almost like old times.

"Louise, I think you like this shit." She gestures at the bruises. "Is life so boring?"

Louise shrugs.

"Puts a glow in your cheeks, does it?"

"Leave my ass out of this." She laughs, uncomfortably. "Anybody ever knock you around?"

"Yeah, my father. To put it politely. You know what I mean?"

"Oh, Kathy . . . I don't think I understood."

"Remember when he died? You were more upset than I was."

"Oh, that's terrible. I'm sorry."

"Well, it's something you put behind you, and you try to move on. Keith, I guess, was a lot like Dad, now that I think about it. See, I've *got* to move on, get away from all that."

"Ohhh." Louise looks sad a moment. "So how is all . . . you know, your plans?"

"Good. Fine. Everything's on schedule."

"You got him?"

"He proposed, I'll say that much."

"Oh, congratulations." She holds up her glass.

"Thanks. Let's wait until you get the invite."

Louise looks skeptical. "Wait, is proposing the same as leaving his wife?"

"He's married almost nine years, Louise. How fast can a man jump? Being fair about it?"

"You tell him about Keith?"

"You kidding?"

Kathy stares at her friend. She's holding herself in an oddly sensual way. Her voice gets quiet when she talks about Keith.

"Louise. I think you want the guy . . . or maybe you already did."

Louise looks away.

"Louise, sweetie. I don't care. It's your funeral. Just get something straight. The guy would fuck a doughnut."

"You can be rough, you know that?

"You don't listen, you know that?"

"So . . . who does?"

They sit in silence for a while. A quiet, sort of timeless feeling in the room. Kathy thinks it could be a room anywhere in America. Anytime when it's light out. Louise squirms on the sofa, says, "So what're you thinking about?"

"What a loser Keith is. . . . The shit I did when I was twenty. It'd turn your stomach."

"Maybe not mine."

"*Alright!* Nurses!" Kathy laughs. "Guys always saying you're hornier than normal."

"We see a lot of bad stuff."

"You see a lot of bodies."

"We see people sick and dying. Anything healthy, well, we appreciate it. Maybe more than most people."

"Great. Well, Keith isn't healthy."

"Are we fighting? I don't have a problem with Keith. You do."

"What?"

"Forgetting you ever knew him. Meanwhile, he's going to be around."

"Really, I do not have a problem. Nada. I see him on my door, I'll have him arrested."

"For what?"

"Anything the man's got on his mind is illegal."

They laugh together again.

"Hell, I'll Mace him. I'd shoot him if I could. It'd be self-defense, wouldn't it? You ought to think along the same lines."

"I don't think I could hurt him."

"Oh, Louise."

"I am a nurse."

Kathy pours some more gin, shaking her head. The bullshit people tell themselves. She's all beat up. Waiting for the next time. What can you do? The only reason Keith talked to her was to get to me. That and maybe getting laid. Kind of sad, but what can you do?

• • •

In the train under the Hudson, going back to Manhattan, Kathy tries to put Louise out of her mind. A lot of heart. A great heart. But look what she's doing with it. And Keith. Put him out of my mind, too. The hell with him, really. Louise still doesn't believe me. I tell her ten times, and she still thinks I'm in love with the guy, because she is. . . .

Kathy thinks back, again, over all the times she's seen Robie. She thinks about the office, the lobby of the building, the streets nearby. Did anyone ever see them together? Did they ever even nod hello to a passing acquaintance, either of them?

Maybe at the very beginning. When they were just chatting. Wouldn't mean anything to anybody. Newspaper people are very friendly. A lot of them drink together. Lots of laughs. Me and Robie chatting, a few feet apart, nobody would look once.

Never once went to my place.

Interesting, she thinks, how careful I was. Not even sure why. Probably some TV program about asshole divorce lawyers. Why give them ammunition?

Thing is, nobody's ever seen us together. That might be important, the way Robie's talking now, maybe doing something extreme. . . . Didn't think the guy had it in him.

Clever, really. Nobody in the whole world knows about

us. Robie and me, working it out, private business, the way it should be.

Kathy gets out at 34th Street, in a good mood. She thinks about going by the office. Then realizes she's probably not entirely sober. Got to be real careful.

She laughs. I see Robie in this mood, I'll scare the hell out of him, for sure. Get him to fuck me in an elevator or something. Whoa, girl. Let's just go shopping.

Chapter 20

Anne goes down the steps into the basement. A delicious tenseness in her whole body. Things you aren't supposed to do . . . why are they so much fun? Well, no, she thinks, not fun exactly. She's nervous, scared. She can feel the beat of her heart. But she wants to do this; she's sharply aware of enjoying it, in a way. It's not just the hope that she might learn something. It's the knowledge—there's a voice in her head saying this—that she's doing something she shouldn't do.

But then you do it anyway, she thinks. You just do it. And there's this odd, sickly pleasure. The way orchids are. They're just too pretty, and they smell evil. . . . Oh well, all my people were Puritans, what can you expect?

She glances at her watch. 6:34. Robert called to say he'd be a little late, he thought he'd be on the 7:07. How many times is that now? She should have been counting, keeping a record. But that was never their style. One of them was always late, or changing things in a minor way. What difference does a half hour make? Or even an hour? Still, she's sure that it's happening more now. Or New York's more chaotic than last year, and editors work more. . . .

I have to start listening more closely to his excuses, she thinks. Never mind. I'm safe now. Coming down here. . . .

It's an almost empty basement, used only for storage. Twenty big cardboard boxes are stacked along one wall. There are piles of magazines and old clothes. They talked about putting a ping-pong table down here, or a pool table. There was always the sense that they'd have children and then the whims of the children would decide what filled this useless space.

The man who installed the recorder looked around and said, "Well, it's getting warmer. Nobody wants a blanket now." He put the device on two magazines, under a half dozen folded blankets. "You don't have flooding, do you?"

She said, "No, never."

Anne stands with her arms folded, staring at the stack of blankets. The odd thing is that she can access the device by telephone, from anywhere. But she worries she'll push the wrong buttons, erase something. No, that's so little of the truth it's a lie. She *likes* coming down here to this musty place. She likes touching the expensive little piece of hardware and listening to what it contains.

She likes, she realizes, the rising anxiety in her chest. The totally alert sense that each second is important, that every sound is something she must pay attention to. The sounds on the machine. The sounds that could come suddenly from upstairs. It's a very long shot that Robert would say he's going to be late, then come early. Still, she knows she is vulnerable.

Anne tries to remember something in her life that combines danger and anxiety and sin, the way this does. She has to go way back. Nothing she did as an adult seems to qualify. There's nothing in college or B school. She thinks about all that hot, clumsy making out when she was a teenager growing up in Ohio. But how sinful is that? Everybody's telling you to do it. All she can think of, really, is when she first masturbated, when she was fourteen, fifteen, somewhere in there.

Yes, she remembers the time with a putter. An uncle—her favorite uncle—played golf and he left the clubs in the front hall. She sat in an old chair and played with his putter. She remembers twirling it. The adults were in a room close by. She could hear their voices; that was a big part of it, the fear of discovery. She remembers how she sat there on that hot summer day, in some loose shorts, and fondled—really, that's what it was—the putter. And then she got the idea of sliding the handle along her thigh, inside the shorts, until the blunt end of the putter touched her underwear. And very carefully she pushed it against her vagina, feeling exquisitely evil, then up higher to her clitoris. She remembers how she leaned forward, covering what she was doing. Still, the putter was sticking out way past her knee. Anybody would have suspected something. She moved it just a little, steady flicks of her wrist. God, she can still remember the turmoil in her thighs, her pelvis, right up past her stomach to her pounding heart. Every few seconds she had to monitor the voices, make sure nobody was moving around. She got wetter and wetter, until she was sure there would be a stain on the chair's upholstery. But she didn't want to stop, she remembers this clearly, she wanted to keep going, going and going, forever. Her body tightened just like a string on her Gibson guitar, everything seeming more shrill and high pitched. Dear God, it was wonderful. The room started to become hazy and brighter. There were probably minutes when the whole family could have been watching, and she wouldn't have known. Maybe they did; and they were always too polite or embarrassed to mention it. Maybe, she realizes, you secretly hope for some horrible exposure, a scandal that proves how truly evil the whole thing is, and how evil you are. But what she remembers for sure is how she struggled with every nerve to make sure nobody did see her. How she stayed with it, cunning and furtive and watchful, and jabbed that putter against herself until a wave of prickly heat seemed to rise through her body. She remembers gasping but trying not to, almost little hiccups. And when the wave passed, she could suddenly smell herself, she was so wet and sticky, which seemed to her the perfect finishing evil touch. She put the putter back and ran to her room. When she was changing her clothes, she realized that her uncle might later smell the putter. The very part he would be holding. Her favorite uncle! She wetted a cloth and raced back to wipe off the putter. The voices still droning in the nearby room. Then she went back to her room again, threw herself on her bed, and thought something like, Gosh, that's so horrible, thanks, God.

Anne is smiling at the details still so clear in her memory. She realizes with a start that she's pressing her thumb against the front of her skirt. Not much, just a subtle accompaniment.

Going to the dogs, she thinks. Robert comes home now, I may attack him. Well, that could be awkward if he's been . . .

She looks at her watch. 6:51. Damn.

She goes back to the steps, listens upstairs. "Robert!" What if he came in while she was daydreaming? "Robert?"

When there's no answer she goes quickly to the blankets, squats down next to the recorder. She plays the voices at a very low volume, just listening for Robert talking to a woman, fast forwarding through anything else, through her own conversations. Listening also to any sounds from upstairs. The whole time keenly aware of the almost sexual pleasure she's getting from all this.

It takes ten minutes to check the last three days of calls. Nothing. Still nothing. And yet she's more sure, just on instinct, that Robert is pulling back from her, drifting somehow, spinning into another orbit.

The bastard, she thinks, resetting the machine, concealing it again.

I really need him now. I wish he would throw me on the living room floor and make love to me. But what if . . . ? I could pull him into the shower, wash him off, like it's a game.

Another woman, she thinks, knowing that she still doesn't really know if there is one. Definitely something evil here. She wonders if the thought excites her even as it repels her. Robert's body still smelly from another woman? Or maybe I don't care. It's Robert's problem. Okay, stud, let's see you do two.

Or maybe trapping him, finding him tired and impotent, is a turn-on. Oh, Robert, that's really a shame, and I thought you were such a man. Getting old, I guess. . . .

Anne goes energetically up the steps, knowing she's on edge and she'd better watch herself. Knowing also she's, by her own standards, getting a little nuts.

So, she wonders, what will fix it? I find for sure that Robert is mine and always wants to be? Yes, that and he comes through the door and tears off my clothes and makes love to me. An Anne Klein outfit?—sure, what the hell!

Or maybe I've got enough time to run upstairs and finish what I've started here. Maybe find a putter. . . .

PART

Chapter 21

They're in a little bar in Astoria, Queens, a ten-minute cab ride on the other side of the East River. Sipping margaritas at 3:35 on a Wednesday afternoon. Nobody they know would be in Queens, and certainly not in a dim, musty dive like this. A cheap motel just down the street.

"Hooky," Robie says. "I love it. Fuck that paper."

They're sitting shoulder to shoulder in a booth. Lots of names and initials carved in the wood table. Hillbilly music on the jukebox. Something about love in a trailer park. Not even five people in the place, counting the bartender.

He turns more toward her, admires her new haircut. Very short, very chic. She looks more like the way he thinks of her. She just wanted a change, that's how she explained it.

She didn't mention coming through the newspaper's lobby on Monday, seeing Keith waiting out front, leaning on his big motorcycle. Not a care in the world, to look at him.

Maybe not a thought either. Kathy studied him from behind a column, then went out another entrance. Glad she didn't feel a thing when she saw him. Or maybe she felt pity for this juvenile delinquent almost turned thirty-five. Or was it anger? Maybe she wanted to go out there and yank him backward over his motorcycle.

Then she thought: *I don't want to look the way he remembers me. For sure.*

"You look great," Robie tells Kathy. "Super." He kisses her. "And terrific. And wonderful."

He pushes her skirt farther up, looks down.

She watches his face. "Like white?"

"On you? Any color they make."

"If you whisper just the right stuff, I'll take them off."

Robie laughs. "Now?"

"For you, lover? Anytime."

"I'm thinking about it," he says. "Love it. No, not yet. We'll ease up to it."

She gives him that lazy fuck-me smile he sees in his dreams.

"Another thing," she says. "I can put a wig on this. Be a blonde."

"Yeah?"

"Might be useful sometime."

Robie nods at her. Pressing his hand along her thigh.

"If, you know . . ."

He shakes his head.

She stares seriously. "I don't know, Robie, it's a big step."

"I didn't think it up," he says sharply. "You did."

"Everything you were saying went that—"

"Drop it, please."

He slides his hand up between her thighs, smiles grimly. "Sorry. Let me put down another one of these Mexican depth charges, and I can talk about anything."

"Or we can go in the bathroom and do something."

"Always thinking."

"Not you?"

"Yeah, I though about it."

She smiles, delighted. "We don't have to think about things. We can do them."

"I was thinking . . . will it always be like this?"

"I sure hope so. . . . Why, what do you think?"

"You know the guys I admire? Cartoonists in the paper. Every day they got to come up with that new joke. I can't even imagine how they do it. Then I thought, well, if what's-his-name can think of something new for Garfield every day, a couple of sex maniacs like us ought to be able to think of some new way to fuck."

Kathy laughs. "Robie, you say the sweetest things. . . . So it *will* always be like this. You agree?"

Robie shrugs. "Looks like it."

"Always and always."

"At least."

She looks the place over, then stands a little off the seat, and eases her panties down. Gets them off her feet, balls them up in one hand and puts the white ball in Robie's shirt pocket. "Close to your heart."

"My *heart*," Robie says dramatically. "Looks like cardiac arrest. It's the margaritas, or that smell . . ."

"You're silly when you drink. You know that?"

"You aren't worried about my heart?"

"You talk about that smell . . ."

"Yeah?"

"I don't want any jokes. I want this expression like, you know, you've gone to heaven and seen the face of God."

They start laughing, so loud even the two drunks at the bar look over.

•••

Robert jogs through Grand Central Terminal toward Track 23. Catch the damned fucking 6:39 to get to damned fucking Bronxville at 7:07. A conductor is yelling something, waving at him. Robert takes a long step into the train, stumbles a little, catches a pole.

Whew. The brain's wobbly, but the legs are weak. The dick's dead. Long live the dick.

He glances scornfully at all the sober assholes who stayed at their desks until 6:30 or some shit like that. Suckers. Let me tell you what I did this afternoon. Funniest thing, I had a doctor's appointment—hey, that's what I *thought*—and the next thing I know this gorgeous nurse starts taking her clothes off. . . . Ah, you couldn't take it.

He sits on the aisle, next to a fat, matronly woman. He gives her a few secret sneers, just to make sure they understand each other.

Now, what time is it, kids? It's sober-up time. By a tremendous act of will. Think sober thoughts, get sober . . . *or*, conversely, just think of a story where everybody got drunk.

See, Anne, this guy got a little promotion, and we had to do the right thing, newspaper-wise. Get drunk and make silly speeches. That's basically the only requirement for my work. Drinking and stupid human tricks. Haha. Aren't you glad you're in a sensible line? You're so lucky! Boring!

He fidgets in his seat, trying to stretch his long legs into the aisle. Arms crossed sullenly over his chest.

Fuck you, Anne. You hear that?

You're not careful, we'll do it. I swear.

He snickers, remembering how Kathy looked at him, said, *Robie, what are you saying, we should get rid of . . . ?*

Well, damn, it sure would make life simpler, wouldn't it?

He thinks about Anne's smug expressions. The way she seems so industrious, so organized. So right on top of things. Everything except what counts. Haha.

The more he thinks about her, the angrier he gets. I married a monster. It's unbelievable.

You think somebody's so nice, so agreeable. But then when love comes to shove, whatever the fuck that is, you see the monster. Monster, monster, monster.

Alright, maybe she'd be agreeable. But I'm gonna take a chance like that? What, six to one, she spends the rest of her life trying to fuck me. All that boring, pent-up energy, I mean, what's it want to do? Find some fucking obsession, right? Anne's classic. I can see right through her. Does the girl bit pretty well. But we're talking gonzo furies inside.

Robert sees in his head a few times he almost told her what he wanted, almost handed her the letter. Then he couldn't do it. Then he thought, No, it's not the smart thing *to do.* No, let's be shrewd about this. Why tell her *anything*? Life is perfect, that's all she needs to know.

Let her think that. Then if something happens to her, she had a good life right until the last second. Right? That's what I want for her. She really loves me, right? She doesn't want to live without me, right?

Basically, Anne's nice. And I like her. If she just weren't such a monster. How could she suddenly be so unreasonable? We always shared everything, compromised, accommodated each other. What happened to her?

I bring this thing up, she'd go right over the edge. Full-time monster. And it'd be my fault. Believe it. Dr. Robie Frankenstein.

I can't tell. What is it most? I feel sorry for her, Anne the boring loser? Or I'm afraid of her, this monster that'll leap out of there? Jesus, I think about it, I just get more pissed. Fuck you, Anne, you hear that?

Robert twists a little side to side, gives a mean eye to some kids who brush against his leg. His head hurts.

It's nuts thinking about it. But what if she did just disappear? Maybe the house blows up one day. I mean, wouldn't that be just the perfect solution for everybody? Even her, really. What do you think, Anne? Come on, tell the truth. Well, damn it, if you'd walk away nice, we could work something out. Why can't I depend on you? That's all I want to know.

Robert realizes it's after seven. Almost there. Drive home with the windows open, get that cold air in the face, get sober. God knows Anne is. Haha.

The train shudders to a stop. Robert gets up unsteadily, moves along with the people getting off. Fucking assholes who died like cattle . . . the machine gun's rapid rattle. Shit, the stuff I used to know. Knew that whole poem by heart. I knew 'em and I wrote 'em. What happened to *that?* Like *New York News* really cares, right? Haha. The readers think Ann Landers is the country's leading philosopher. Yeah, ha, I guess she is. Dear AL, what should I do with my boring wife who's in the way? Oh, you don't like *my* idea? Well, fuck you, too. So you made ten million telling saps what to think. I'll do it myself, thank you very much.

In the station he sees himself in a mirror. Whoa, check this guy out, looks a little used. He focuses his eyes, stares at details from his hair down to his jacket. Alright, like I said, a little party, gee, Anne, wish you could be there.

Robert goes out into the parking lot, taking deep breaths, slapping his face several times. Just don't want to do anything stupid.

Maybe like slap Anne a few times. Woman makes me so mad.

Yeah, that's funny. I think I'd enjoy that. Slap her around, rip her clothes off, make her crawl around on the floor naked, begging. Say something nice, sweetie. Nice and dirty. Woman needs somebody to wake her up, sort of what Kathy did for me. Hell, who wants the job? Hey, you. . . . Guy in his Paul Stuart togs. You want my wife? You're probably some kind of pervert anyway. You like doing it by the numbers? My wife's in taxes. Haha.

Robert leans against the fender of his car, watching one car after another pull out. The headlights scything through the dark.

Funny thing, thinking about somebody else fucking your wife. Man, it must be over when you don't care. Kind of sad.

Other hand, what the hell isn't? He laughs darkly, gets in the car. I got a lot to think about. . . .

He gets out of the car, takes off his topcoat, throws it on the seat. He walks back to the station, finds a phone, calls Anne.

"Hi, honey. I'm right here in the station. . . . Yeah, Bronxville. Car's acting funny. Probably flooded it. Tell you the truth, we had a little party at the office. Don't worry. I'm almost back to my normal pedestrian self. Anyway, didn't want you to worry. I'll give the car a rest, then be on my way. Everything cool?"

"Sure. You want to eat out? Or come home?"

I already ate out, Anne. Haha. "I'd like to just be home, tell you the truth. Nothing fancy. You mind?"

"No, no. Take your time."

"Lovely. See you."

Good thing, be a little drunk, think about whether I could really do it. And what's the best way. Then think about it when I'm sober. Get things all clear in my head.

He sees her there in the house, probably the kitchen phone, wearing one of her work outfits. One of those double-breasted numbers, which makes *four,* if you ask me. Hey, she's entitled. The Monster of 114. Got to take care of her.

Funny, something so way out, and after a while it seems completely reasonable. Like, let's drop our jobs, move to California, live a new, silly kind of life, don't think so much, make things out of seashells. California! Nuts, right? Then you start working out the steps so you could change your life around. And after a while, hey, you're thinking about what color to paint the new den in fucking Pismo Beach.

Just have to be smart. Work out the details. Do it.

He walks slowly across the now-quiet parking lot. Enjoying the chill in the air, knowing it'll help use up the alcohol.

Seriously? You think you could do it? Yeah, that's the scary part. I think I could. Don't like to think I'd enjoy it. That's sick. Alright, don't touch that. We're talking, do or not to do. As a practical matter, as the only sensible thing to do. Say a guy's got some old parents, worth ten, twenty mil, he's got to think about it. Sure, just some little accident, some little anything. Life goes on. Yeah, that movie where the plane crashes in the Andes, I think. A bunch of guys ate the dead guys, got through it. They made such a fuss about it. Wimps. You're starving and there's meat there. What's there to talk about? The best cut, that's about it. Haha.

Robert stands by his car, watching the cold creep under his skin. He feels a few goose bumps, then he shivers.

Hey, I'm feeling pretty good. What a day. Kathy and I get married, she'll probably kill *me*. Good cause, I guess. Like Dylan says, ramming that green fuse through the something. Can't remember. Everybody knew he meant screwing.

Robert gets in his car, a four-year-old Toyota, and starts it up. Everything he looks at seems very vivid. Everything feels possible. Sure it is. Is this America, or what? We're heading out, going west. Man, it's a good thing she found me when I'm still young. Long trip and you got the fucking Indians up there in the hills. They're always spread out along the ridge. Pretty. I wonder if that's the way it was.

He drives out of the parking lot, onto Kraft Avenue, for the run home. Go see the Monster in her lair. Hi, Anne. What a busy day. Glad to make it back in one piece. You have any fun today? No? Gee, that's a shame. Things kind of dull? Don't worry. We're going to take care of that.

He rolls his window down, lets the wind chill his face. For I'm a seafaring man, by heck. I am, I yam. . . . He remembers that people get numb permanently, sitting in a cold wind, but there's the house up ahead. Too late. I'm disfigured for life. The Humpface of Bronxville. Now we'll find out who really loves me.

He pulls in the drive, nudges up against Anne's Volvo. Uhhh, how's that for a little bump in the night? Buy American, you asshole. Oh, that was funny. Cabdriver from hell.

First time I touched Kathy's breasts. The next thing you know I'm marrying her. . . .

Robert gets out of the car, stretches, and walks across his lawn. Looking up at the shape of his house, the sky beyond. Nice. The stars up in the sky . . . are like a big pizza pie. Jesus. How's that go? Oh, moon!

He unlocks his front door, shuffles into the living room, making a lot of noise on purpose. "Anne! Honey! I'm home. . . . Hell, I smell LIKE BEER . . . take a SHOWER."

He hears her voice but he's bounding up the stairs and can't make out the words. What a pro. "Just a MINUTE!"

He gets in the shower, soaps himself all over twice, goodbye Kathy. Then he grits his teeth and turns up the cold for thirty seconds. Ohhhh-fuck. All done in five minutes. He puts on some casual clothes, dark blue cotton sweater, tan corduroy pants, bounds back down the stairs. His thick hair still damp.

He finds Anne in the kitchen, smashing a head of lettuce. "Hey," he says, "you really get into that, don't you?"

She smiles at him. Good old sweet Anne. He goes over and touches her arm, kisses her cheek.

"Just relax," she says. "Everything's done."

Robert sits on a counter, swinging his feet. Smiling sort of dumbly, telling her he's really a nice guy, not up to anything bad, just trying to earn a living with a bunch of crazy drunks.

He watches Anne, looks her over. Nice healthy figure. Just a sweet person. What is *that*, ohmigod, some nipple? And look at that face! Who could hurt . . . ? Forget it. No way. I'm trapped here forever. Monster and me, and baby make three.

Anne crumples the big head of lettuce.

Robert grimaces. What am I gonna do? I'm A-1 stuck. A thousand years from now we'll still be here, Anne making little salads, me drooling on my tie.

"You know what we ought to do," he says.

"What?"

"Some night, just get wrecked. When'd we do that the last time? Years ago."

"Now?"

"Oh, no." He laughs. "I did it already today. . . . Just some night."

She gives him a pleasant look. "That sounds good to me."

There, he thinks. Sweet. What can I do?

It was always like that. You'd go in a crowded room, and you wouldn't see Anne right away. Then you'd feel this sweet presence, sort of lurking somewhere. What the hell is that? I feel something. No star face . . . not tits . . . not ass . . . What the hell *can* it be? Ohhh, it's Anne.

"Great," he suddenly says. "Good cheap therapy, that's what I always say."

"You do?"

"Somebody does. I thought it was me. Maybe not. Well, it's the thought that counts."

"And the proof."

"What?"

"The proof, Robert. Like ninety."

"Oh, right. Riggghhhtt." There, you see. Sweet and real funny.

Chapter

22

Anne leans back at her desk, staring at some figures that don't make sense. Lunchtime coming up.

She thinks, I don't feel like eating alone, impulsively grabs the phone.

"Edd, hi, Anne. You want to have lunch? . . . I didn't talk to you for a while. . . . No, let's go out. My treat. . . . About twenty minutes? Fine."

Twenty-one minutes later he comes to the door, wearing another dark suit and white shirt. He knocks softly, says, "And away we go." Then he smiles. Well, for Edd, it's a smile.

They go down to the lobby, then outside. A bright April day, sharp shadows everywhere, a slight breeze. They walk along enjoying it, not saying much, Edd his usual low-key self. She'd forgotten how much so. He sharpens her sense that Robert really has changed . . . gotten looser and noisier and, she's not sure, somehow more adolescent. She's trying to put this into words when Edd says, "By the way, you remember that case the boys were talking about?"

"I'm sorry."

"Month or two ago. We had lunch in the cafeteria. This guy shot a burglar."

"Oh, yes, I remember."

He glances at her, waits until he catches her eye. "I took care of it."

"Edd . . . what do you mean?"

"I made a few calls. Made sure the guy's lawyer knew what's what. He won't have a problem."

Anne walks in silence for a while. "Edd. Maybe you'd better explain this a little more."

"Let's just say it's a favor."

Anne blinks. "But why?"

"I saw it bothered you."

"You mean you pulled strings?"

"Anne, come on. I can't pull strings. I'm nobody. Let's just say I intervened in the system, minutely and anonymously. I wasn't going to mention it."

"Well, that's . . . extraordinary."

"Not really. Took twenty minutes."

She studies him for a moment. "But you, you personally, don't really care one way or another?"

"It's no skin off my nose."

"But the firm's pro-bono work—those boys, as you put it—you undercut that."

"I decided your reaction was valid. Did you change your mind?"

A curious man, she thinks. His tone doesn't suggest that he cares whether she has or not.

"No, Edd, I didn't. . . ."

"It was the right thing to do, Anne. So I did it. No big deal."

"As a favor to me?"

"Basically."

"But you weren't going to mention it?"

"I just wanted you to know it's history. By the way, the same group was in there last week. They are so wonderfully cynical. You almost have to laugh or cry, depending on your temperament."

"And you?"

"Like I said, it's no skin off my nose. I just listen. They had some more war stories. Good ones. Want to hear?"

"Let's get some lunch first. Maybe a glass of wine."

"Good plan. By the way, Anne, how are you?"

"Oh, fine, Edd. Everything's fine."

"That's good. Well, winter's gone, for sure. Pretty soon we can move on to what really matters."

Anne smiles. "And what is that?"

"Anything you do in hot weather. I really ought to live in Arizona. But if it's hot all the time, you don't appreciate it. My father always said the changing of the seasons is what made all of civilization. Sad to say, people in Arizona are quite a bit slower than here. There's a corollary there."

She's conscious of grinning at him in a silly way. "Really, Edd, you make me laugh."

"Goes with the turf," Edd says blandly.

"Oh, here. . . . How about this place?"

"Looks good to me."

•••

Anne sips the last of her wine. Can't allow herself more than one glass. The numbers will start dancing. She studies Edd now and then. His glen-plaid suit, the plaid so subtle it might as well just be a gray suit. The nondescript tie on a white shirt. Short, well-combed hair, almost black. A haircut that always seems about a week old. Sensible, ordinary male features. Never raises his voice, or even inflects it. Hardly ever laughs. A man you barely notice, she thinks.

Then he orders the kind of lunch a kid would. And he's got opinions on everything. If she encourages him, he'll talk nonstop for five minutes. And if she doesn't, he sits there.

Watching her? She's not sure. Waiting for something? Apparently not. A very self-contained man.

"So why," she asks, "are those young men so cynical, do you think?"

"Lawyers have always had a reputation for cynicism. You'd be amazed at some of the comments people made fifty or a hundred years ago. And of course there's Shakespeare. 'Kill the lawyers.' Almost four hundred years ago."

"But isn't it worse now? The cynicism, I mean . . . or am I getting old?"

Edd shrugs. "You're not that old. Yes, it's probably getting worse. Lot of social engineering in our schools these days—I think it just makes the smarter kids into cynics. The people who do the engineering usually aren't the brightest; they don't even notice what's happening. Look at Russia. Corrupt idiots at the top, two hundred million very bitter cynics underneath."

He's finishing off three scoops of chocolate ice cream, with chocolate sauce, digging out the last bit of goo with a long spoon.

"I guess you like chocolate?"

"I'm a chocolate kind of guy."

Anne laughs again, not meaning to. "Uh, you said you had another story."

"Maybe it's not that interesting. I'll make it brief. This man gets lost in Yonkers. He's on a side street. Two young men approach him. I don't know the details, but basically they beat him up, rob him, kick him. And the whole time they're laughing, calling him names. 'You stupid asshole.' Excuse me. So this guy is half dead and mad as hell, probably out of his mind as well. He sees this pushed-in fence, a vacant lot, I guess. He reaches in for a brick. He gets to his feet and lunges after them. One turns. But, guess what, he throws the brick, hits the other one in the back of the head. That's important. The mugger drops and his buddy runs. So what does our guy do?"

"Can he walk? . . . I don't know."

"He screams for help, then he waits for the police to arrive. Then what does he do?"

"I think I see. . . . He tells them what happened."

"Every detail. Trying to be helpful, you understand. When they asked him what he hoped to accomplish, he said, get this, 'I kept wishing I had a shotgun, so I could get both of them.' "

"He waived his rights?"

"On video. The mugger died, by the way. Brick hit just right, cracked his skull."

"Well, that's too bad. But surely our firm is not representing either one of these muggers."

"Of course not."

"Well, that's good."

"The dead man's daughter. She's suing for child support. Through law school, one assumes. Of course, the police have no choice but to charge the victim with murder. Et cetera, et cetera."

"Edd . . . the way you tell this. You don't care? And don't say it's no skin off your nose!"

Edd shrugs. "What can I do?"

"I'm asking how you feel."

"Don't you see, Anne? Our government doesn't always protect people, but it always gets very annoyed when you do it yourself. That's where we are now."

"So what's the answer?"

"Well, the victim in this case could have done ten things differently, and he'd be in the clear. He was trying to be a good citizen, he thought. Basically, he's going to trial for being old-fashioned. Or, if you prefer, stupid."

"Oh, Edd. That's so . . . cynical, isn't it?"

"I'm sorry you say that. I didn't make this world."

Anne messes with her napkin. "I'm curious now. I'll ask Robert—my husband—what he thinks about it."

"He's with a newspaper, isn't he?"

"Yes, *New York News*."

"It's a good story. That's how he'll see it."

Anne suddenly feels very sad. She's sure she remembers a more idealistic world. But perhaps that was long ago, when she was a child, and she saw the world in a very shallow way. Or maybe it's Robert, and she's on edge because of him. Solely because of him.

She's sure now about the other woman. She keeps hearing the brief message again and again. Robert called, got her machine. A bright, cheerful voice—"Sorry, not around. You know just what to do." And Robert said, "Yes ma'am, I sure do. I just couldn't resist saying hello. Anne's out shopping. Miss you." And a click.

And there it was, what she'd confidently predicted for weeks, what she'd told herself to expect. It's still a jolt.

"Anne, really," Edd says, "I just try to understand things. . . . I'm sorry you're upset."

She stares at him, not sure what he's talking about. . . . Oh, the muggers.

"No, Edd . . . I was thinking about something else."

He nods agreeably, as if he's not surprised by that or much of anything.

•••

As she drives home that evening, Anne thinks, If he wants out, why doesn't he just say so? . . . If he doesn't want to be with me, I'm not going to hold him.

She mulls over this, driving along Thurmond, catching a light, speeding up again.

Well, maybe he can't decide, can't make up his mind.

She laughs bitterly. Oh, I'm still in the running, am I? Is that a plus? I should dwell on the little hope left?

Or I should just cut my wrists now? Just get out of his way, one way or the other. Is that what the good wife does these days?

No, the good wife gets a lawyer and you go to court and

learn to hate each other. I wouldn't do that. I make as much as he does. Well, that's not the point. I just wouldn't want to end on that note.

She stares at the sky. Still some light this time of night. She realizes her vision is fuzzy, that she's crying. Well, damn it, I love him. I'll always love him, I think.

She thinks once again about the woman's voice. Sort of sexy. Very confident. Young? Well, definitely younger.

Anne imagines her husband with this other, younger woman. . . . Tough to do. Not a good thing to *try* to do.

So what's the sane response? I give up? Or I fight back, try to keep him? I don't know. . . . If a friend asked me about something like this, I'd be lost. I am lost. That's the point.

She thinks about the words, "Miss you," the way Robert said them so sincerely. Maybe passionately. Unless that was some little private joke. Sure, he talks to people at work like that.

Miss you. Miss you. Miss you.

Now she's crying like a child with a bloody knee. How can I go home like this? How can I go *anywhere* like this?

She wants to pull over, wait a few minutes. She's afraid someone will bother her. Or a friend will recognize the car. It's almost completely dark now. She's not ten blocks from her house. Just concentrate on the road, she tells herself, drive slowly.

Kiss you. Kiss you.

She remembers driving in a heavy rain, hardly able to see past the front of the car. Leaning over the steering wheel, peering at the street. It's like that now, but when she blinks hard, clears her eyes, the street is suddenly sharp.

Oh, yes, Anne, she mocks herself, you're the unluckiest person in the world. Nobody else has problems. Oh, the hell with everybody else. I'm feeling sorry for me now. I *need* to feel sorry for me. I need to cry for a half hour, then go on with it. Then maybe I *can* go on with it.

She pulls over and stops just short of the turn that puts

her on her own street. Worried about her neighbors seeing her like this and, simultaneously, thinking that this is such a pathetic thing to worry about.

And if you don't change your underwear, that's the day you'll have an accident—and everyone will know. Yes, Mother.

She bangs her forehead gently against the top of the steering wheel. What do I do? That's all I want to know? Just push on. Tough it out. Maybe it's a phase, a whim, a passing thing. Already falling apart of its own weight, from Robert's guilt, and his love for me.

Miss you. Miss you. The way he said that . . . sounds like it's all over for me.

You're a fool, Anne. What's worse—failing at something or just being a damned fool? I'm sure I'm both. I can't get away from that feeling.

She looks up, stares at the various houses and lawns she can see. Unevenly lit and shadowy. Still, she feels safe. A safe neighborhood, safe people. Only her own house, she realizes, isn't safe. So who *protects* me?

She turns on the interior lights, twists the mirror around so she can look at her face. Ohhh, a mess. Red and streaked. What can I tell Robert? I ran over a squirrel and it upset me? I had a fight with the bitch in heat who's my boss? I got a sad phone call. . . .

Isn't it something? All I can think about is making sure he doesn't know what I'm really crying about. This is the part I don't get. It's his lie and I end up participating in it. He works to keep the lie going, and I'm right there working with him. I smile, say, how are you, nice day, how's the paper, did you hear what the President said . . . ?

His lie. Now it's my lie. But what's the way out? I say, Robert, we have to talk.

Is that the worst thing? That I look him in the eye, say, You lying bastard? I could do that—if it came up. But bring it up? I don't see how.

That's where I started. I don't want to precipitate any sudden changes. I'm terrified of that. I'm sure, somehow, the whole thing is really my fault. Then, if I shake things up, maybe destroy the marriage, then it's doubly my fault. Is this making sense? I can't tell anymore. . . .

She's wiping away streaked mascara, fussing with her makeup. Trying to decide if she's presentable enough to venture home.

Maybe, she thinks, it's time to fight back. Go home and do something wild. Maybe pull his pants down and attack him. Funny, sex is good all this time. He's sort of rambunctious, to use a neutral word. Maybe I could challenge him, the way he thinks about me.

Sure, Anne, you're really up to doing something wild. What can you do that's wild, without going to pieces at just about the same instant? Nothing, that's what.

She turns the key, starts up the car, continues around the corner.

I'm paralyzed, that's what I am. She realizes this now, and feels it like a weight on her chest. It's not sad, she doesn't cry again. No, it's strangely static and unemotional. What can she do? Nothing. She can do nothing.

"Sounds good to me," she says. "I can't do a damned thing. . . . *Hi, Robert! How are you?*"

She pulls into the driveway.

"Did you have a nice day? And how's the paper?"

She sees them greeting each other. Everything just like it always was.

Chapter 23

He lies on his side, his whole body tense, watching her intently in the soft light of the room. He touches her head, enjoying the feel of the short silky hair. He tries to be perfectly still, let her do everything, draw it out. Then the pressure in him seems more like pain than pleasure. He can't hold back; he hates the thought of this ever ending. He stares at her lips, then he thinks about Anne, sees her saying something, *Please, Robert, don't.* . . . No, block that. Jesus. He wants to say something to Kathy but he can only gibber a few disconnected syllables, gasping and snorting. His body tosses, stiffens, shudders. Ohh, Jesus, what . . . oh, wait . . . no, keep on . . . oh, that's so . . .

He sighs and lies still. After a long silence, he still can't think of the right words. He seizes her shoulders, pulls her up close to him, hugs her hard, whispers in her ear. "Wow. That's wonderful."

She whispers back, "I'll say." She pulls her fingers through his hair. "When things get boring at work, I imagine you're sitting on my desk in front of me. You and what's his name."

He lets that go. He feels almost normal by now. "You say bored? Everything okay in marketing, isn't it?"

"Sure. We're carrying the paper."

"What?" He snuggles close to her, running his hand along her side and over her hip.

"Every week we've got some new gimmick." She pulls back and smiles at him. "Hey, you don't think anybody actually reads the thing?"

"I know they do. Look at the pissed-off letters I get."

"Couple of people," she says. "The rest play the games. The April Fool's Four was mine. Moi."

"You've got the magic touch." He pinches her lower lip.

They laugh together.

"We ought to talk some," he says. "Want to sit in the shower?"

She rolls off the bed. "Good plan," she whispers. "Like the spies do. Robie, you know what stories you ought to be doing?"

"What?"

"About the schools, making them better."

"Why'd you think of that?"

"Silly. We're going to have kids, aren't we?"

Damn. "Yes, right. I see. . . ."

They go in the bathroom, Robert carrying a Heineken by the neck. Kathy turns the faucets, feels the water. Robert sits at the other end, his legs drawn up. She thins the spray, then settles down by his big feet. Her chin on his knees. Robert watches the water splattering off her head and shoulders. Water streaming down her face. She smiles at him through the hot mist. "Short hair's nice," she says. "Saves a lot of time."

He holds her shoulder. "You look great . . . I love you."

Really, she looks impossibly great, he thinks, and I do love her. And that's the beginning and end of it.

"You better, you better, you bet—"

He can't imagine giving her up, and he doesn't want to disappoint her. He hates the thought of somehow not measuring up. "Well, one thing . . . I did check, uh, on the insurance. . . . A lot of money. It's been in place almost five years. So nobody would connect it to us."

"I see. That's kind of grisly." She thinks about it. "But I guess it's a factor."

"You bet. Three hundred thou. And another hundred thou in the paper's benefit package."

"Huummp." She shakes her head. "Well, waste not, want not, I guess. . . . Robie, can you go through with this?"

"Yes, I think so. Right now I don't see any other way." He shrugs uncomfortably. The spray is making him squint. "Like I told you, we've got to think about the practicalities. Weigh the pluses and minuses. That's what I've been doing. The insurance is a big plus."

"Go on."

"Conversely, you have a messy divorce, you lose that *and* a lot, lot more. So instead of four hundred thousand up, you're a hundred thousand down. A half million bucks! Maybe decisive all by itself. Then there's the wear and tear of the thing. Sure, there'll be wear and tear this way, too. But it'll be on our terms and it'll be over soon enough."

"All I know is this, lover. If you're in, I'm in. It's terrible, but I think somehow it'll be a kind of sacrament. If we do it together."

"Because . . . we'll be doing it for each other."

"Yeah, putting everything on the line for the other."

Robert grimaces. "Let's don't talk quite like that. If we do it right, there's nothing on the line."

"No, I don't mean just the risk. I mean . . . it's a kind of sacrament, isn't it? I mean, like a ritual. We give up one person so two others can be happy. I don't know. Look, it's not a little thing. It's a big thing."

"One person who is very much in the way. I get angry

thinking about that. Then I know I can do it."

"We do it for each other, Robie. Anger is secondary."

He thinks about what she said. "Good, you're seeing clear on this. Great! Alright, another thing that seems clear to me is that, and you've already agreed with this, we have to do it ourselves."

"I always thought that. I don't know why. Well, it's a sacrament, like I said."

"Kathy. Remember that little bar in Queens? The first thing I thought when we walked in. That's the kind of place people go to hire hit men. They think! You can't believe how dumb people are. But there's a story once or twice a year in the New York papers. Some wife wants to get rid of her husband. She goes in that kind of bar, whispers to the bartender, I need a tough guy for some dirty work, you know what I mean. The bartender says, I've got just the guy. Only he turns out to be an undercover cop. The wife makes a down payment, sixteen cops jump out of the bushes. And she's in jail for a long time. And he's free."

Kathy nods. "I have read that. Yeah, some things you have to do for yourself. That's what we're saying. Both saying."

"Here, let me stretch this leg." He kicks out the right one. "A year ago, maybe you remember, this business guy actually tried to hire a private detective. I couldn't believe this moron. He's maybe fifty, successful, and he thinks he can walk into a detective agency, put some money down, and the detective—a guy who's licensed by the state of New York, who's got references and credentials—will kill people. And the plan!? Broad daylight, at a store. Shoot an extra person, make it look random, like a botched robbery. I read this story three times. A year ago. It just fascinated me." He smiles at her. "Maybe I saw something coming."

"Smart man." She massages his leg some.

"You just can't bring other people into it, that's the point. You might want to. But the very people who're out there, looking for this kind of work, are the dumbest, most unstable, most unreliable people imaginable. Unless you get a real pro. Then you're talking a lot of money. And the Mafia owns you forever. Forget it. They'd blackmail you for every dollar you have left."

"This is nice," she says softly. "Sitting here in a warm shower. With the man I love. Falling asleep. It's that protein . . . it makes you sleepy. . . ."

"Don't fall asleep. I'm telling you all this so you can poke holes in it."

She yawns and then stares at him. "We do it. We do it together. We do it alone. Agreed. That's as far as you got. . . . And we do it for each other. That's important."

He holds her face between his hands. "You're so smart. That's why I feel it's a sure thing. Two smart, savvy people . . . we can figure something out. Right?"

"Hell, if we can't, lover, nobody can."

•••

Robert goes down first to the bar. It's on the sixth floor and looks out over Broadway and 52nd. The hotel caters to Europeans. Hell, Robert thinks, you hardly hear any English in this place. Great.

He settles in the most secluded booth he can find, waits for Kathy. Thinking about what they did, what they said. He's still on edge. Or maybe it's a high. Now he has to worry about somebody seeing them. Hell, let it happen, he thinks. Funny thing about danger. You start to like it. Just bluff the assholes. Shhh, can't talk, we're looking into a new French connection, know what I mean? Mum's the word.

Robert looks over the bar, the people. He likes the shadowy, foreign feeling. Yes sir, we're in the Big Leagues now. Things look pretty solid to me. Poor Anne.

When the waitress comes over, he orders two gin martinis.

Kathy comes in five minutes later, wearing the tinted glasses. Hell, she could be French. Looking very chic these days. She sees him without looking at him, waits for him to signal it's okay. He touches his right ear and she veers slightly and makes her way toward him. God, the woman is cool. What a partner. What couldn't she do?

Kathy slides in next to him, winks. "Hi, lover. Funny meeting you here. You come . . . here a lot?"

They smile at each other.

"Seriously," Robert says, "we are not doing anything here."

"First anniversary," she says. "We'll come back, wake the place up." The martinis are already there. She sips hers, leans close to him so they can talk in whispers.

"You got it, sweetheart. So look, the trip idea seems right to me. I'll mention it to her, sort of drift into it. I can't tell her where, that might seem loaded. I'll throw out a bunch of ideas, tell her I'm real tired, need a rest. Wherever we go, we'd be there two days. Plenty of time for you to catch up. I keep thinking Bear Mountain would be perfect. Get alone somewhere in the woods and, what do you think, we're attacked by this little mountain guy in a pea jacket."

"That little guy is going to shoot you, too, you know. Have to."

"Ouch. Yeah, you're right."

She kisses his face. "I'll do it with love."

"I'm not thinking about that part. It's your job. Alright, it's just a question of settling on some place. This weekend, the one after. She might say Boston; she's got a sister there. Or I might say, no, let's be alone, pick somewhere you've always wanted to go but we never did. I let her set it up. Look, I think it's a walk. Things don't work, we wait, try again. The main thing is doing it right."

Kathy listens, thinks he's got it. Some fake toughness maybe. But he's dealing with the details, really thinking about them. Going to kill his wife for her—her and a small fortune. Still, it's the long way around. But, hey, that's about as far as a man can go. I think about it, I get hot. Always a good sign of being in the right place.

Kathy licks his face. "Together forever."

"You got it."

What a thing, Robert thinks, looking down at her face. If anything, the fever's growing, not dropping off. The more I get, the more I want. Sounds like love to me. What wouldn't I do for her? He feels unbelievably strong. Hell, he thinks, I can do this. I can do anything.

whatever. No fucking on the roof angles. No cunt-crazy-editor-kills-wife stories around here.

God, just thinking that put a shock up my rib cage. Am I losing it? I am losing it.

He ignores the new reporter in the elevator and as they rush out to Third to hail a taxi. He smiles to himself as she has to run to keep up. He gets in the cab first, sliding to the left side, yelling instructions to the driver. "*Come on*, Ferguson." He waves her in. "We're going to the front lines."

She sprawls in, trying to please. He stares straight ahead, a rock of an editor, planning all the big stories he'll make out of this second-rate disaster. Actually seeing Kathy bending over in front of him, slowly hiking her skirt. . . .

"Mr. Saunders?"

He looks around at her sincere face. The dark hair has a smooth, shiny texture, like Kathy's. *"What?"*

"Is everything all right?"

"Of course. What do you mean?" Who the hell is this, Florence Nightingale?

"I . . . you don't look so good."

He stares at her in a belittling way. "Yeah, Doc? So how do I look?"

She tries to smile. "Like, you know, somebody who's seen a ghost. Sorry. I don't mean literally. My mother uses that expression."

Robert presses his hands over his face, and then through his hair. His skin's a little damp. Christ. Is it that obvious? Is it the sex I'm getting? Or the sex I'm thinking of getting? Or what we're planning. . . .

"Ferguson," he confronts her, "this is a rough business. Lot of stress. Things sort of peaceful in Rochester, are they?" Always put down the cow towns. Only one New York. Etc.

"We're starting to get a lot more murders," she says. "If that's any indication."

Robert almost laughs. No, give her the steely look. You, little lady, will never measure up in this man's eyes. "Makes you proud, doesn't it?" He gives that a David Letterman grimace.

"No," she says seriously. "I hate it."

"Hmmmmm." A little whippersnapper and, what do you think, she wants to take the high moral ground. And mother me in the bargain. Look like a ghost, huh? No, Ferguson, it's Anne who's going to look like a ghost. Haha. And by the way, would you like to hear some of the things I did in a cab recently, me and Kathy? Gross you out. Or, if you're a lot more hip than you look, stick you to the seat. Haha. I could show you . . .

The cab passes 28th Street. He hears sirens not too many blocks away.

"So you're all right?" she says, looking at him with this concerned expression. For a second he thinks it's Anne.

"Damn it, Ferguson . . . Lucy. Drop that. Ask me something to do with newspapers."

"I'm in the business four years, Mr. Saunders. I think I'll do a good job for you."

Robert almost says, "Don't count on it," but loses heart. Ferguson is the type you can't pick on. They don't notice or they burst out crying.

The cab swings left and stops near 24th. The street is barricaded. Three cops waving traffic away. Robert sees masses of people at midblock and beyond them a thin wall of smoke four or five stories tall. He pays the driver and gets out on the left.

"Okay, show time."

She gives him a tight, military nod. If she were any more fucking businesslike, she'd creak. Bitch'll probably have my job in a few years. Damn, what a thought. Maybe I'm going too fast. Everything's going too fast. Yeah, but I'm in control. I am, right?

Robert holds his ID out for a cop to see. "*New York News.* She's with me. What's the situation?"

"Worst is over, I guess." The cop nods them through. "Almost put a car in a tree, though." He smiles. "Might be a Guinness."

"They didn't evacuate the block?"

Cop shrugs. "People who did it said it's okay now. You trust 'em?" He gives Robert a look—I'm glad I'm posted here, that way when the street blows up again, you'll be dead and I won't.

Robert gives him a disapproving stare, doing his Ferguson imitation.

"Come on, Lucy. Like I said, the front lines."

"Yeah," the cop says after them, "see if you can make ConEd surrender. Hahahaha."

They walk east on 24th. Robert sees fire trucks, maybe ambulances, on the far side of the smoke. Several cars are parked at odd angles. Most of the people here are cops and other reporters. At least a dozen photographers. Medics in white clothes. Robert looks for faces he knows, finds two of his own people. He chats with them for a few minutes, turns to see Ferguson scribbling in her notepad.

"New kid on the block," Robert says. "Do something good, or she'll get your desk."

They all stare toughly. The smoky air stinging their eyes.

Robert grabs one of the reporters by the arm. "Listen, Owen, beside this, you got the Nash story. Don't forget it."

The man gives Robert a funny look. "Boss. We went over all that day before yesterday. You got Alzheimer's already?"

Robert realizes the man is right. A little awkward. "I want to keep you on your toes," Robert says with fake good cheer. Jesus. "Hey, I got a lot on my mind. Ecological collapse and, guess what, my fucking in-laws—you know what I mean?"

The reporter laughs. "Oh, I know. Seriously," he whispers, "I know you got something on your mind. Be careful."

"No problemo, pal." Jesus! Robert breaks away, signaling Ferguson to keep up. They get closer to a big hole along the south curb. A hole big enough to put a minivan in. Some ConEd guys working in there, cops pushing the photographers away. Robert looks up at the nearby trees, finds one with broken branches. Damned explosion pitched a car up there! This city'll get you, one way or the other.

They jostle past people. Everybody trying to move someplace else for a better look. Robert and Ferguson work along on the north sidewalk, closer to the thin smoke, which is drifting slowly eastward. They step between parked cars. Robert sees forms on the asphalt, the injured. No, two of the bodies are covered. A medic comes out of an ambulance and goes to one of the forms, lifting the sheet for a moment. Robert glimpses a woman's face, very bloody. Blond hair with red splotches in it. Roughly Anne's coloring. The little he sees of the face looks similar, too. Damn.

He turns away, bringing his fist to his mouth.

Ferguson is right there, watching him. "You all right?" she says. What a maddening person.

"No, damnit. Woman I used to . . . be in love with. Dead."

"Oh, I'm so sorry. Oh, Mr. Saunders, forgive me."

Once he gets the reaction he wants, he relents. Shakes his head, smirks a little, to indicate he's not entirely serious.

He turns away, toward the drifting smoke. No, it's too fast, that's all. Everything's happening too fast. Look what we're talking about, for Chrissake. . . . No. I've got to slow this down. What is it, three, four months? I know it's what I want, it's right. But come on, we don't have to run a hundred-yard dash on this thing.

In his mind he sees the dead woman. Yeah, he thinks, she's just lying there. Not moving again. All over for her. That's what it means, jerk. She's dead. Yeah, and Anne'll be . . . like that.

He takes a few deep breaths, watches how scrambled his thoughts are. Not good. Got to be cool. Hell, cold. Otherwise, forget it. Got to slow down. Tell Kathy it's the only smart thing, make sure we're completely clear on this thing. She'll understand. I hope she'll understand. Damn. What's that she said the other day? "I've invested a lot in you, Robie, because I *believe* in you." Oh, yeah, now I'm a god. Sure. Absofuckinglutely.

Ferguson's at his elbow. "I've got an idea. Let me bounce it off you."

Robert looks hard at the green irises, then into the black pupils. Maybe make some kind of impression. "Yeah, I'd love nothing better."

Alright," she says, missing everything, "here's the angle. . . ."

He hardly hears a word she says. Nodding vaguely. Seeing Kathy in his head, taking off her clothes. Seeing the dead woman. Seeing Anne as he raises the knife, fires the gun, whatever it is, something final. Thinking how much he needs a drink. Telling himself, Nod, nod at this crazed rookie. Meanwhile, imagine Kathy's perfect breasts, they're so reassuring. Almost hemispheres, really remarkable, and these red grapes. . . .

"Mr. Saunders . . . you all right?"

There, just when he's about to kiss the nipples, *there she goes again.*

"Ferguson, damnit, people are dying around here. Let's have a little respect." Yeah, woman, let's shut the fuck up sometimes. Just for the novelty of it.

The young reporter stares at him, bewildered. Her face going from one uncertain expression to another. "Well . . . I'm . . . uh . . . sorry. . . . Did you really . . . recognize somebody?"

Robert tries to look haughty. Damned rookies—*when will they learn?*

Now he tries a laugh. "Yeah, kid, I saw a ghost. Haha. Just like you said."

She looks away. Wondering if he might be crazy. He sees this in her face. Right, I might be. Crazy for pussy. Crazy to think some of the things I'm thinking. What about crazy in love, that's not so bad, is it? Love justifies a lot. Helen of Troy, what was that all about? Some guy crazy in love, right? No, two guys! Just like me. One of them carries her off. I get that! The other one takes a whole army to get her back. Let's go, soldiers—a woman like this, we don't mind dying, do we? Dying or killing, what's the difference? You do what you have to do. . . . But maybe not so fast. That's all I'm saying. Kathy, I love you. Do not doubt me. But, look, it's no good to run off half-cocked. We do it like pros. Careful, meticulous. That's all I'm saying.

Robert makes a point of watching some cops hassling a reporter from another paper. Pretending to react to this, when all he's reacting to is his thoughts. He finally turns back to Ferguson's obnoxious presence, says, "Hey, lighten up. That's a good idea. You'll do fine."

She smiles, relieved, still watching him curiously.

"Think I'm a little nuts, right?"

"I'm . . . not sure what to think."

"Yeah, well, sister, do five years in this crazy town, and then tell me about it. That a deal?"

She nods with a faint smile, accepting the challenge.

"This place chews people up and spits them out. Watch yourself."

"Thanks. I will." She relaxes. They're in this together.

He can tell she likes that. Good luck, little Lucy.

"Now, what we'll do is go to a bar, get drunk to inaugurate your lofty new position in the world of higher journalism, write your story up on some napkins, make you famous. That's the first thing the gods do if they want to chew you up."

Robert laughs darkly, figuring he's got her mind pretty well fucked up, so it's a good day. She won't be putting two and two together, that's the main thing. And he can go back to thinking about Kathy's nipples, the way she says, "Now suck this one. . . . Ummm, nice. . . . Now this one," holding them out to him.

"Mr. Saunders?"

This woman! With a pathetic sigh, Robert says, "*What*, Lucy?"

Chapter 25

Anne's standing by the large window in the firm's reception area, apparently looking down into the streets of White Plains. Actually thinking about some things Robert said on the tape. Thinking about them again and again.

Edd walks into the reception area, sees her profile, stops. She's totally preoccupied. He watches her for a minute or two. Then she turns slightly, or she feels his presence. They stare at each other.

He studies her with his bland, all-knowing expression. Or his know-nothing expression. With Edd you can't be sure. And how long was he watching her?

"Oh, Edd," she says as casually as she can, wondering if she needs to invent an explanation. She feels flustered or violated or vulnerable. Emotions, in any case, she doesn't want to feel. How could she possibly tell him what she was really doing?

"Hi, Anne," he says, his voice low and neutral. He moves closer to her side, glances out the window, says, "There an accident or something?"

"No, no." She decides not to bother with alibis. Then she adds something that is true. "I've got a few minutes to kill. We're going out to dinner." Never mind that he'd expect her to work at her desk until the last minute. Well, *she was*. Then she started out, and for some reason stopped to stare out the window.

"Right. Where're you going?"

"Carter's, I think. Nice place."

"Yes, it is." He stares into her eyes, shrugs. "So, everything's all right?"

"Oh, sure." She smiles, thinking what a colossal lie that is.

"Can I walk you down," he says. They stand uneasily for a moment. "Unless there's more time to kill."

"No, no," she laughs, looking at her watch. "All killed."

They walk to the elevator. Anne wondering if she could confide in this man, maybe use his judgment? That's been a problem. Whom do you trust? After the first sentence, everything's out in the open. In particular, her life, her heart. She can't seem to find a way to confront Robert or ask him or tease him or sneak up on the topic from any direction at all. How's she going to mention it to her mother or her roommate at Wharton or her other friends . . . or this quiet, aloof man? No, she can't, that's the answer.

"So, Edd, how's the bridge game?"

"We're wininng a lot against the local talent. But I don't suppose we'd amount to much against the big boys."

"Well, how do you know?"

They come out of the elevator, start across the lobby. "Ahh, it's like any game. The higher you get, the more it's a game of inches. Then quarter inches. Finally, there's some bastard beating you by an eighth. You play twenty hands and you're neck and neck. Then there's this hand where if you can count every card, you can win on a squeeze play.

But with the pressure and not seeing where it's going, you're down to a couple of cards, and you can't place the seven of diamonds. So you guess. Fifty-fifty, right? But this other guy *knew*."

Anne stares at him. "Sounds rough. You keep reliving it the next week?"

"Yeah, I do. . . . Same in pro football, tennis, whatever. You can't ever let up. You do, and the other guy doesn't, it's over. Another thing. The people who get to the top really want it bad. Maybe they cheat. In bridge, I mean."

"Oh, don't say that."

"There's a lot of borderline stuff, anyway. What they call card sense is partly the psychological signals that players give off."

They go out the revolving doors, Anne thinking about people giving off signals. Outside, in the soft light of dusk, she asks, "Can you read them?"

Edd laughs. "Does a gentleman read somebody else's mail?"

Anne stops. "You do, Edd, or you don't?"

"Anne, I've been playing with this one woman for a couple years. Almost three. I know things about her she doesn't know. I mean at the card table. She has these very tiny mannerisms." He laughs uneasily. "When things get tight, I start watching them a lot more closely."

Anne blinks. Just what she's doing with Robert. But why isn't she any good at it? I've got to get better, she thinks.

Edd misreads her expression. "I hope this doesn't shock you."

She's glad he misunderstood, plays on it. "Well, Edd. I'm pleased that you are concerned."

He sighs. "I know some of your mannerisms, too."

Anne stares again. Intrigued by this, then abashed. The intimacy of the comment unsettles her. "Well," she says lightly, "I won't ask for examples."

Edd does something funny with his eyebrows, raising

them a few times. Anne smiles. "Good night, Edd."

"Bye-bye, Anne." He walks away toward his car.

She watches him a moment, his lean, straight form, then turns the other way. Glad they're going out to dinner with Sam and Marie, comfortable friends. Get out of the house. That house where they both lie so carefully, all the time apparently.

Anne shakes her head as she walks. She has never thought herself capable of even small lies. As for the man she would marry, complete honesty was always the first requirement. Now look, all of that turned to dust and nonsense. She is lying every minute, what other way is there to put it? She knows about Robert and this woman named Kathy, but she pretends not to, pretends to feel about him as she always did. Well, maybe she does. Robert, meanwhile, is in love with this Kathy, not her, but he pretends their life together is exactly as it always was. Exactly. Unchanged by an eighth of an inch. How big a lie is that? As big as the world, she thinks.

As she slides into her car, she thinks again of the tape. "Kathy, uh, I can't do it now." The most interesting words she's heard in years. They sound negative, defeated. There's a setback, she feels. And she wonders again what *it* is. And for the twenty-fifth time she comes back to the word *divorce*. How horrifying that Robert has even contemplated this. But how wonderful that he can't do it!

She's trying to think clearly about this. Knowing it's almost impossible for her. He's leaving me, he isn't? She's tossed about between these extremes. I'm living, I'm dying? I'm rich, I'm bankrupt? Who, she wonders, can think clearly about such chasms?

Anne drives the two miles to the restaurant where she's meeting Robert and the other couple. As she pulls into the parking lot, she thinks: Yes, but I'm not bawling like a baby. That's a change, isn't it?

She remembers the several times she almost crashed the car—from not being able to see through her tears. Oh, my God. Just to think about it appalls her. She was going completely to pieces, a nervous breakdown right on the highway.

She's ashamed of herself. Some cop would look down at the wreck and say, Just like a woman. And what could she say in response? Oh, you big brute, you just don't get it, do you? Yes, that would tell him. Right.

Anne laughs for a second. Yes, she's a little cooler now. Definitely. But what does that mean, really? Your heart is dying? You don't care anymore?

Well, I know the worst, and I'm still here. Somebody named Kathy. They're . . . doing it. There, I said it, almost. She laughs again, although faintly.

She stares at the front of the restaurant. Insects circling in the lights over the door. She's a few minutes late. But not enough to matter.

Really, Robert amazes me. That's the main thing. That he could do this, and then pretend he isn't. Do I even know this man?

She gets out of the car and carefully locks it. She starts toward the door. Robert, Robert, Robert, she thinks. Who are you? Who the hell are you?

•••

Robert orders a second bottle of wine. Sam swirls an almost empty glass, goes on talking. "Business is good, I tell you. The President says X, everybody assumes he means Y. Buy! BUY!!"

Anne watches Robert, to see if he reacts to this. My husband, the liar.

"Then later, they wonder, maybe this time he *means* X. No, sell! Goddamn it, SELL! I tell you, I love this guy."

Marie suddenly excuses herself and leaves the table. Sam gestures after his wife. "She's upset." He shrugs sadly. "You know, about having children. Three beautiful Irish setters we've got. They aren't enough. We were arguing coming over. I guess I shouldn't talk."

Anne stares after the other woman. No, she hasn't seemed happy all evening. Anne guessed what was going on.

Then Sam smiles at them. "But you two. What a couple. I really have to say it. You're so nice to each other."

Robert leans playfully against Anne's shoulder, places his hand over her arm. "Well, thank you. Hear that, Anne? We're a model couple."

They stare at each other, and then slowly lean together and kiss. Anne experiences the whole thing very slowly and vividly. Robert's big earnest face, all that hair, the full mouth, his eyes steady as their lips touch. Or are they steady? Robert flicking his tongue in—what?, to make sure she feels his undying passion for her? Anne wondering if she's misunderstood everything. Sam has, or she has, that's for sure. Why can't I just ask him, say, "Robert, what do you *want?* What are you *doing?*"

Sam watches them with an approving grin. "See what I mean?" he exclaims. "I love you guys." He reaches out excitedly for their hands. "Marriage is tough, but you two are naturals. . . . Me, I don't know. Poor Marie."

Anne wonders if she could just blurt it out, maybe that's the answer. Drink some more wine, pretend to be a little tipsy, say, "Robert has a little secret, don't you, Robert?" Like it's a joke, a silly thing, but keep the pressure on until he has to blurt something himself. "What's the secret's name, Robert? You can tell us. We're all good friends." Maybe, she thinks, maybe I can do it. . . .

The waiter comes with the next bottle, fills all the glasses. Sam raises his briefly. "Here's to you lovebirds." He gulps down some more wine. "Hey, you guys are leading me astray. Ever think of that? I don't even drink." He stares in surprise at his glass.

"This might be the night you make a son," Robert says, winking at him.

"Oh, bite your tongue. The child would be a wino." Sam laughs merrily.

Just blurt it out, Anne tells herself, then see what happens. . . . Oh, why is it so difficult? Anne remembers her mother's friend, the one with a strange smell about her, and how her mother could never say anything. "You have to," Anne lectured her mother, "for her own good. You have to. Maybe it's a medical problem. Just do it." It seemed so easy. . . . Anne laughs at herself. Sure, it's always easy for *someone else* to do. And that was just this odd smell. Not a marriage, a whole life. . . . No, do it, stumble into it.

Anne makes a show of sipping rapidly from her wine. Get a mood going, some momentum. Maybe somebody will say, "Anne, you're drinking a lot. . . . " Give me an opening.

Marie comes back slowly to the table. Holding herself somewhat stiffly and apart. Anne feels sorry for her.

Then she laughs at this. Oh, Marie, if you only knew about me! If you could hear what your crazy husband just said! Robert and I are naturals?!

Anne finds some last bit of asparagus on her plate, pushes it with her fork. Watching Robert in furtive glances. I married him. I thought I knew him. Now I wonder what he's capable of, and I don't know.

"Desserts," Robert says, looking around the table. "I saw something on the menu. Chocolate suicide. Now, how can you resist that?"

Anne remembers how Edd said, "I'm just a chocolate kind of guy." An odd thing for him to say, she thought. But maybe, she thinks now, I'm no longer a good judge of what's odd.

"Yes," she says, "I'd like a dessert. You, Marie?"

I'm not all that angry, Anne thinks, surprised. I'm not sad. Not mainly. So what am I? Right now? . . . Paralyzed? . . . Yes, that's true. And I'm . . . *curious.* Yes, I'd like to know just what's going on in my own damned life. Is that so unreasonable? I'd like to know who this man is. *I've got to know.* It's now or never.

A waiter is sticking a menu in her face. She takes it with an irritated grimace.

"Marie," Sam says loudly, "they're getting me drunk. Anne and Robert. Can you believe these guys?" Again he reaches for their arms. "I love these two."

Marie watches his grasping hands. They're not grasping her. She sighs heavily. Anne sees her friend's eyes mist.

Darn, Anne thinks, Marie's got the real problem here, the for-sure problem. No, I'd just upset her more. . . . I can't start a scene now. It wouldn't be right. I have to comfort her.

Robert looks out across the restaurant. A successful man, energetic but at ease with life, that's how he appears. With his stylish suit, the blue-striped shirt, the somewhat grand manner. Anne thinks about them going home. They'll undress and lie down together in bed. Maybe they'll kiss good night, maybe they'll do more. Just like any other night. It all seems so bizarre and strange to her now, like odd customs in far-off places, something you read about in an encyclopedia. She stares at Robert's eyes, the set of his mouth, utterly fascinated.

He can't do it *now?* Well, when can he do it? And, if he does, how will he do it? How will he leave me? Kindly and gently? Or will he say, Drop dead, Anne, you're history. I'm out of here.

Anne sighs gently, wipes her mouth with a napkin, trying to conceal the agitation in her mind. That's what's fascinating, she realizes. I don't know any answers. Nothing. The screen's a blank. Her mouth feels dry, and when she tries to make small talk, no words come to mind. Yes, poor Marie, stare at her, look concerned, the men will think that's what I'm worried about. Keep going as if life is normal.

Chapter 26

"Yeah, I've got somebody," Kathy says.

"Well, what's he like?" Stephanie says, leaning forward eagerly. "Well?"

Kathy smiles distantly. "You want to get all excited?"

Stephanie, a friend from work, shrugs and strokes her drink. "I wouldn't mind one bit." She laughs. "Until the real thing shows up."

They're at a little table in a bar on East 63rd Street. Noisy after-work crowd, mostly standing and milling around. Men in suits, women in office clothes, everybody grinning and talking a lot. Kathy isn't about to tell Stephanie about Robie. But she can't be too coy, either, or Stephanie will figure it out, maybe make lucky guesses.

"He's in Philly," Kathy says with a little sigh. "A management consultant. He comes up most weekends."

"So, it's serious? Or do we smile at these guys?" Stephanie

carefully scans the room. "Nice place. Some good material." She snickers, looking back at Kathy.

"Let's play hard to get," Kathy says. Trying to keep Stephanie in low gear. Kathy figures this is the kind of woman who'll spill a drink on the first thing in pants—"Oh, I'm so sorry, let me wipe that off."

Stephanie frowns, goes back to stroking her glass.

Kathy feels just a little down. Disappointed, really, although she tries not to think that word or feel that emotion. She glances briefly at the faces of the men, just to see if there's any reaction. Remembering that first time she saw Robert Saunders, how she knew right away. She remembers the exact words she thought then. *That's the one, that's the man.*

I always had good instincts, she thinks. Never had any reason to doubt them. I see something I want, I know it's something I really want. But that's only half of it. Something I want, something I *should* have. For my sake, for his sake.

Kathy shakes her head, smiling at her thoughts. Damn, I have to say it, it almost felt religious. Like it's our destiny, and God wants it, too. Now, who could I tell *that* to?

Stephanie brightens. "Oh, come on, you're getting off on something. Give me some."

Kathy smiles in a bored, worldly way, as if Stephanie couldn't really be ready for her beautiful memories. Well, most of them are. Until Robie started to . . . what's the word . . . waver?

"No," she says, in a softer tone. "I miss him, that's all. You don't have anybody, huh?"

Stephanie tries to joke. "I'm here with you, aren't I?"

"Maybe I'll bring you luck."

"I'm ready for some of that." Stephanie sighs heavily. "Tough being a girl in this city. You ever think about leaving?"

"Not now."

"It's crazy here. Half the guys want to mug you, rape you, something bad. And the other half want to talk about your clothes. *Seriously?*"

All he has to do, Kathy thinks, is tell his wife he wants out. That's it. But no, he's got ten reasons why they have to do it the hard way. Okay, I'm in. Then he's slowing down on that, too. I can't do it now, he says. We have to make sure everything is just right, he says. Everything what?

Kathy finishes her drink, gestures to a passing waiter. *Another one of these.*

"Me, too," Stephanie shouts.

What's Robie doing, really? Running in place? Backing up? Damn, I hate to think that.

Kathy feels a tightness along the ribs on her left side. She reaches down for her purse, something to do. She makes a big deal out of finding a five.

No way I could be wrong. But, damn, that's how I know for sure. He does what he has to do.

Kathy grimaces, working to the end of this. . . . If he won't, then he's not the man I'm looking for.

She sits back, her face blank.

"Let me guess," Stephanie says. "He said he wouldn't come in your—"

"No," Kathy says, trying to laugh. "I *told* him to."

"Oh, now we're getting somewhere."

A man in a blue suit, a yellow tie, holding a beer against his chest, stops by their table. He's got a big smile. Kathy almost snarls at him, almost says, "Take a hike, asshole." Then she sees Stephanie's face, the way it got warmer and happier. Kathy makes herself look down at the table, let Stephanie do what she wants.

"Well, a talent inspector," Stephanie says gaily.

Kathy hears their voices, and she hears Robie saying, "Not now. I can't do it now."

What? You doubt me, Robie? I am yours totally. What is the problem? That's what I just can't see. If you're the man, you have to act like it.

"And who's this?" the man with the yellow tie asks, smiling down at Kathy.

"Sorry, buddy, I've got a headache."

"Oh, well, maybe we can fix that."

She gives him a cold stare. "Don't push your luck."

The guy laughs uneasily, turns back to Stephanie.

•••

Kathy leaves the bar a little after ten. Three drinks tired and ready to watch Arsenio for a few minutes and fade. Maybe give Mom a call, see how she's doing. Kathy walks down Third, careful to glance behind her now and then. Still a lot of people about. It's reassuring, but she has her right hand in her coat pocket, holding the little tube of Mace. The city, she thinks, that never sleeps, and never weeps much either. Some cabbie gets shot every day, some cop, some guy in a deli. Governor says the death penalty sends the wrong message. Yeah, and his message is we don't care who gets killed. Hell, I'm just down now. Oh, Robie, Robie, Robie, you're letting me down.

Kathy reaches the corner of 51st. What a great three months, she thinks. Wouldn't trade it for anything. Maybe it's over. Maybe it's all bullshit. Hell no, it's good. Not everything goes all the way, turns out perfect. Man, it takes two to do the nasty. She smiles grimly, walking closer to her building.

She stops. *And there he is.* She's still sixty, seventy feet away. Never mind. She knows the way he holds himself, the pretend-lazy posture. She stands and watches him. He's not even looking around. Just staring up at the building across the street, smoking a cigarette. Leaning on his motorcycle. Worked with Louise, why not her?

What the hell, she thinks, it had to happen. She shrugs, starts toward him. She walks quietly up beside him, says, "Hello, Keith. And how are you this lovely evening?"

He turns slowly, as if he's not surprised she's there, as if he always expected her at just about this time. He grins at her, a handsome, crooked grin. "Hi, babe. How're you doing?"

He's got on the same leather jacket she last saw him in. The black hair's shorter, more styled. There's stubble on his face. He looks her over carefully, finally settles on her hair. "Whoa, look at you. Miss New York! Looks good."

"Thank you."

He straightens up off the bike, stretches briefly, faces her. "It's good to see you. Real good. The feeling mutual?"

The light from her building is shining on his face. Oh, he's a man, alright.

"No, Keith. And you know it. You going to waste my time pretending you don't?"

He snorts at that. "You think you got over me, pretty Kathy?"

"As a matter of fact, I have. I'm sorry, Keith. We had some good times. That was then. Don't make me be rude to you."

He looks up at the hazy dark sky, a few stars there. Takes a last puff on his cigarette, then snaps it in the gutter. "Boy, we did have some times, didn't we?" He smiles at her. "You know what I keep thinking about? That night we climbed up the water tower. Great big old mushroom thing. And we got right on top, and fucked half the night. Joking how all that shaking might make the thing fall right over." Keith laughs. "Ain't that just something in this world? You had guts, babe. You always had guts. I'll tell you the hard truth. There's nobody else as fine."

He reaches out to touch her arm. She backs away one step.

He smiles easily. "I got plans, Kath. Big plans. I want you with me."

"Any of them legal?"

"Yeah, all legit. Mostly. You'll like 'em."

She isn't sure how to talk to him. Man's like a tide. "Keith, please listen to me. As far as you're concerned, I'm a dead woman, I don't exist. You have to accept that. You keep hanging around, I'll call the police. You're probably on parole or probation or something, right?"

"Ain't no never mind, babe. Thing is, you're fooling yourself, you think I'm out of your system. Hell, you haven't forgotten one bit of it. Remember how you used to wake up hanging on to me? Like I might get away. *Don't ever leave me.* You said that a number of times."

Yeah, she thinks, I did. What a guy this is. Not really that big, just wiry and mean. Keith almost never got in fights, people didn't want to mess with him. She wonders if he's right, even a little? Not out of her system? She looks at his face. The nose almost comes right out of his forehead. Dark eyes, full mouth. Yeah, a tough guy, she thinks. But then there's this little bit of mischief there, too; he sees the funny side of things. That's the part that hooks a woman every time.

He winks at her. "You still miss me, right?"

"No, Keith."

"Say what you want, pretty darling . . . I know you do."

"I'm tired, Keith. I've got a real job, a good one. I need a lot of sleep to do it right. You've got to stop this."

"I know about your job," he says. "Good show."

Kathy starts to shout at him. She notices a couple approaching, lets them walk on past. "History, Keith. Ancient fucking history. Our life together. Get it? That thick skull. What is in there? Anything at all?" Yeah, that is the problem, isn't it? Man's just not that smart. "You listening to me?"

"*Listening?* Every pretty word, babe."

"Keith, you want me to start screaming? Throw a fit right here?"

Keith looks puzzled. "What for? What's the point? I want you back. You want it, too."

The man's wearing me out, she thinks. What am I—tired? angry? Hell, I married him, once long ago. Hate to be mean to him. Thing is, *ouch*, Keith wouldn't pull any of this shit that Robie's doing. Look at him, comes right to my door, lays himself on the line. I say, Keith, go over there, break the door in. He says, Sure, babe. Keith, beat that guy up. Just take a sec, babe, be right back. Keith, drop that old lady you got at home. Sure, babe, it's done. Yeah, she thinks, staring right at Keith, I'm angry, angry with Robie. Oh, poor, dumb Keith, I really am history. I've outgrown you. How can I explain it?

"Keith, what do you want? Right now?"

He smiles. "You. You and me."

Kathy frowns, wondering what she's going to do with this guy. The cops and lawyers and all that aren't very reliable. How could she trust them? Besides, he hasn't done anything, really. You can't just tell Keith anything. . . . Hell, she decides, I have to do it myself.

"Look, we'll go up, have a beer, talk this through for the last time. You've got to understand. It's over. You know my name. That's as close as we get. Forever."

He's grinning. "Sure, let's go up."

"Are you listening?"

"Always, darling."

No, he's not. Kathy shrugs, turns toward the door to her small, walk-up building. He ambles along behind her. She unlocks the first door, gets three pieces of mail from the letter box, then unlocks the second door. There's a small lobby, white walls with two paintings, and stairs going up.

"Third floor," she says.

"Show the way," Keith says. "I always liked walking up steps behind you, you know that."

"Yes, I know that."

"I been all over, Kath. Ain't nobody as fine as you."

She sighs. "Thank you, Keith." Thinking about Keith watching her ass, wishing it were Robie. Wishing he were coming up behind her, grabbing her some way, hell, fucking her right on the stairs, saying in her ear, It's done, pretty lady. We can get married today, go to Bermuda for the weekend. That good for you? Oh, you bet. Oh, what the hell are you waiting for?

They walk along the narrow hall, stop in front of 3C. "Home," she says.

Inside, Kathy points to the little dining table. "Have a seat, Keith."

He looks at her, almost smacks his lips. "Sure 'nough." He goes to the table, throws his leg over a chair without pulling it out, settles confidently in.

Kathy takes off her coat, then sits across from him. "I was just wondering . . ."

"Yeah?"

"What can I say to make you understand that everything's changed. I've changed. The river moves on, Keith."

"Maybe so. But we can ride it, too." He grins. That beautiful dumb grin of his. "Like a king and queen, darling."

"No, we can't. Believe me."

He scowls and smiles, letting the little lady have her say.

"I've gone on, Keith. I've outgrown you."

"Easy to say"—he smiles—"hard to do."

Kathy stands up. "You want something?"

He shrugs. "You got that right."

"To drink, Keith? To eat?"

Still not the right question. Keith grins at her.

"Keith—how about a beer?"

"Thanks."

"Maybe some bacon and eggs."

"Now you're talking. You didn't forget my favorite meal. Not counting, you know—"

"Keith. Let go." She walks around to the small kitchen alcove. She turns on the water to make some noise, give her a moment to think. She looks back at her ex-husband's profile. He's sitting there, or slouching there, one arm on the table, cool as ever, smiling to himself. What is he thinking about, Kathy wonders. Other than fucking my brains out.

She opens a cabinet, pulls out the small frying pan. Then she goes to the refrigerator, finds the eggs and butter. Keith glances at her briefly, says, "You're looking real good, Kath. Glad to see you in fine health."

He seems to mean this. She picks up the frying pan and

moves behind him. She lifts it back over her right shoulder, holding it with both hands, twisting the handle until the pan's flat bottom is facing forward. Then she swings the pan like a baseball bat, in a smooth, horizontal arc right into Keith's head. The noise is surprisingly loud. He slumps over on the table.

She shudders at the sound, then hits him again. "That one's for beating up Louise."

Kathy puts the frying pan on the sink, goes to the phone, dials 911. Hears the bored cop voice.

"Hi, this is Kathy Becker." She gives the address and phone number, slowly, precisely. "My ex-husband came over and started hassling me. I hit him with a frying pan. He's out. But he might come to. I want some cops over here right away. My life could be in danger."

"Sure thing, lady." Cop sounds happy now. This call sounds real, not the usual false alarms and bullshit they have to listen to all night. And on East 51st Street, no less. "Fast as we can."

She sits at the table, across from Keith, to wait for the cops. He's breathing heavily, but breathing. She doubts she could kill him with a frying pan. Head of concrete, this guy. But she could knock him out. That much is for sure. Look at him. Wasn't anything to it, she thinks. How long's it take to raise the thing? He's sitting there thinking how we'll be jumping in the sack after the bacon and eggs, I guess. I was wondering how to do it. I kept thinking it'd be difficult. Wasn't. It was nothing.

She reaches in his jacket for his cigarettes. Still a Marlboro man. Should've known. She lights one, inhales at length, exhales slowly, staring at Keith's face. "You come to," she says, "I'll hit you again. So don't."

She watches him some more. "I'm not betting any big money," she says. "But I do bet you get it now. You just needed a clear picture. A real big, real clear picture."

She feels better now. Dealing with this thing. Hell, she

thinks, dealing with anything always makes you feel better. It was so easy. She sits back, smiling some. "Tried to tell you, old buddy. The river moves on. And you," she laughs, "well, you sink to the bottom."

She thinks about Robie, wishes he could see her now. See, man, it was nothing. I was soooo cool. Pressure? What pressure? You just do it a step at a time. One, two, three. . . .

The buzzer sounds, she gets up to let the cops in. It's sweet, she thinks. Tell them everything just the way it happened, but then just at the end he got mean, she was scared. Better check his name on the computer, guys. Oh, yes, I'll press charges. And why did I let him in? He said he wanted to talk. Why not? He used to be my sweetie.

She stands by the door, smiling. And me just so damned pretty. With a fancy job and great tits. Who's going to believe Keith about anything?

Man could've listened to me. Paid just a little attention to what I told him. Hell, then he wouldn't be Keith, would he?

There's knocks on the door. Kathy glances at Keith, then down at her blouse and skirt. She notices the cigarette, shrugs—hell, I was so scared, guys, I really needed one, you know how it is. . . .

She opens the door, lets two cops in, a man and a woman. "Oh, officers," Kathy says, a little breathlessly, "thanks for coming so fast. . . . There *he* is. . . ."

She does such a good job, the big male cop reaches for his gun as he rushes in.

Chapter 27

Kathy is waiting in front of a little shop on Water Street, peering in the window now and then to look busy. She's wearing a light tan coat and sunglasses. A few minutes after five a cab pulls up and Robie gets out. He's got on a similar coat, a gray tweed cap, and the sunglasses Kathy gave him two weeks ago—"your secret lover glasses," she called them.

Kathy starts north and Robie falls in behind her. The big stone rampart of the Brooklyn Bridge is ahead. Robie stares at it, wondering what she's got in mind. "A surprise," she said. An excitement in her voice he hasn't heard the last few weeks.

The air is cool for late April, but the sky over the rampart is a bright, cloudless blue. It looks like a summer day.

Kathy walks to the steps leading up to the bridge. She glances back a few times to smile at Robie. When they're on the walkway, she slows down, lets him overtake her.

"Well, lover—what's the good word?" She wraps her arms around his neck and kisses him. Their sunglasses click together.

He wants to ask what's going on, what they're doing down here. Instead he gives in to her mood, her exuberant physical presence. She doesn't just kiss him. She has this way of flattening her belly against him, and sliding her breasts subtly side to side over his chest. Here, she seems to say, feel those nipples, they're hard because I'm glad to see you. . . . Now, where's that hard dick, aren't you glad to see me?

Truth is, he thinks, I always am, desperately, sadly, wildly happy to see her, to feel her against me. That's just the problem. . . .

They pull back and stare at each other, trying to see through the dark glass into each other's eyes. She's grinning, making little kisses with her lips. "What a beautiful day, huh? It's a great day, I can feel it. A lucky day. Come on."

"You're in a good mood," he says.

She doesn't let him ask any questions. She seizes his arm and they start walking toward the center of the huge bridge. Cars going by on a somewhat lower level, with a continuous roar. Far below them and off to the right is New York Harbor, a shining expanse of hard blue-green. Here and there white ships slide through the dark water. The sun still well up in the western sky above the gray smear of New Jersey. When they look in that direction, the sky seems bright and gauzy. It's hard to find the small spire that is the Statue of Liberty. The farther out they go, the more they feel the breeze slap their faces. In the center, they seem to be a hundred yards up from the water. Surrounded by a complexity of steel and speeding traffic, and beyond all that the stillness of the surrounding blue sky.

"It's wonderful, isn't it?" Kathy says, hugging his arm with both her arms. "The whole world around us but all alone." She nods at the few other pedestrians. "Well, almost. I thought about wearing this blond wig I got. Then I thought, Who do you know that actually walks across this thing?"

"It's funny . . . I never did. I was on the Circle Line a couple times. Parties and such. And you go under this bridge and you think, I've got to get up there."

"And you never do?"

"You never do. It's a long walk, for one thing—"

"Great! It's a first. I was hoping it was."

Kathy wondering what would be more spectacular than the top of a water tower, and she thought of the Brooklyn Bridge. And she thought, Yes, that's it. We'll do it in the center of the damned Brooklyn Bridge and I'll tell Robie I've got it all figured out.

"You're in a good mood," he says again. "What's going on?"

"I'm just so glad to see you." She stands in front of him and unbuttons her coat. Watching his face. She takes his hand and places it over a breast. "You know what we're going to do?"

His head recoils an inch. "I'm almost afraid to ask."

"Don't be afraid. Be happy. I've got it, Robie. I *know* what to do now."

What a radiant smile, he thinks. Where's she get the confidence? He feels her fingers on his fly. He glances to the side, find out if anyone is walking by. Two men coming but still a long way off. He stands even closer to her. Yeah, what difference does it make? With their coats open, who can see what's going on between them?

"Oh, you do?" he says, kissing her nose. Both hands now covering her breasts, massaging them slowly. Now and then spinning the heels of his palms over the hard nipples.

"I *do*, sweetheart." She reaches in his pants. Almost laughing, she goes on, "I've got the whole world in my hands."

"And what," he asks, trying to match her playfulness, "are you going to do with it?"

"No," she insists. "What are you going to do with it?"

He's not sure how to respond. His face turns questioning. A look she doesn't like to see.

She slides her hand under his hands, unbuttons her blouse. "It's one of those hook-in-front jobs." With one hand she unhooks it, pushes the bra aside so he can see her breasts. Down between them he can see her other hand sliding on his prick. "I'll tell you, Robie. . . ."

They're silent while the two men walk on by.

"Robie, we are here on this solemn occasion, before God and man, to fuck. And to celebrate the beginning of the rest of our lives."

He recoils minutely. "What?" Fumbling with her breasts, trying to watch everything, feeling the pressure of her fingers, feeling breathless, not in his body exactly, in his head, he thinks, sensory overload. What's she mean she's got it all figured out, she *knows* what to do now? Trying to keep up with her is hard work, Jesus, look at this woman, such beautiful red nipples. . . .

She nods at the lamppost they've stopped by, at the base of it. "Move me over there. . . . It's a bridge, Robie. It goes from one place to another. That's—what do you say?—poetic or something, isn't it?"

She steps up on the base. Now they're eye to eye. But he's not staring at her eyes, but down between them. At how she's stroking his prick with one hand, easing her skirt up with the other, tucking the hem in her belt, tugging the panties aside, steering his prick up inside her. "There," she says, with a sigh and a smile of triumph. "Fucking on the Brooklyn Bridge. Hey, Mom, look at me now. Do it, lover. . . . Don't *worry*, Robie. People'll think we're just grinding. Who thinks anybody's fucking in the middle of this old bridge? . . . Bet it's happened a *million million* times before!" She's laughing now, leaning so close their glasses are an inch apart, saying, "Fuck me, my good man. Now and forever. Everything is A-O-K."

Robie tries not to glance at people that might be coming,

tries not to think of what's they're doing—*We're on the Brooklyn Bridge, for God's sake*—but to focus, concentrate on Kathy's body, all the wonderful parts of it, his body in hers, that almost animal smile on her lips, the little dirty things she says suddenly and randomly, her ass in his hand, her breasts he's tossing around just below his chin. Go with her, Robert. Fuck with everything you've got. Not big strokes, just little strokes. Who can tell anything? . . . Damn, man, just see if you can keep up, in any sense. . . .

"Grab me harder," she hisses at him, "hurt my ass. Oh, yes, yes. Get in there. . . . Now if I could just figure a way . . . to suck you at the same time, we'd have it then, wouldn't we? . . . Nice, baby, nice. . . . I'm dripping all over the fucking bridge." She laughs maniacally.

•••

"Oh, shit," she mutters. "Oh, wow. . . . Great. . . . You think anybody saw us?"

"Didn't you look?"

She smiles. "I was quite busy. . . . Let's just stand perfectly still for a few minutes." She hugs him tightly. "Don't ever leave me," she sighs. "Whoops, it just left me. Actually, I was watching your face. When you came. It's a kick. It gets all scrunched up, like this." She imitates him, which is funny and vaguely unsettling. "I'm just gasping like a horse, right? Somebody drowning?" She laughs softly, not waiting for an answer. "Hell, I was. *Drowning* on the Brooklyn Bridge." She screams: "Hey, people, figure it out! . . . Hey, is that my spit on your lapel? Sorry. Robie, having a good time? There"—she zips up his pants—"all proper." She glances down. "Wish I could say the same for me. Jesus, mister, WHAT have you done to my tits?"

She fixes her clothes, says, "Come on. We're walking to the other side. Get a drink at that bar there." When Robie glances back toward the skyscrapers of Manhattan, she says: "No, no. We have to go all the way across. It's part of the ceremony. Fuck in the *middle.* Go *all the way* across. Got it?" She grins at him. "Besides, there's thousands of people back there watching with binoculars. Probably better if we don't let them see who we really are."

"Damn." Robie shrugs uneasily. "You are so up. . . . Alright, we go across. You going to tell me what's . . . going on?"

"I told you. I got it all figured out." They're walking now.

"Go on."

"You love me, Robie? You want to marry me?"

"I do. You know I do."

"So tell your wife what's happening. Or if you want to go the other route, I can handle it myself. You have to do something, you know, a token. I have to have that. But the fact is, I could do the whole thing without you. I know that now."

Robie looks at her with a startled, almost frightened expression. "Kathy, how do you know that?"

She smiles, swaggering a little as they walk along toward the lower skyline of Brooklyn. The bridge sloping down now. "I just *know.*"

"Damn, Kathy. Tell me. What happened?"

"Details aren't important." She hesitates, figuring how to play this. "Look, Robie, I don't want to upset you. Don't ask for details. The short version is that this guy bothered me, in the street, you know. Mugger, I guess. And I handled it, Robie. I looked at this guy, and I thought, Fuck you, buddy. And I knew what I had to do. Just saw it in my head. How to talk to him, how to stand, how to act. I was completely cool. And I said I thought I had another ten in my pocket and I put enough Mace in his face so he's rolling on the ground. And I walked away. And I thought, Yeah, I can handle the other thing, too."

"That's amazing," Robie says with awe in his face. "I mean, wonderful."

"If that's what you want to do, you got it. My gift to you, Robie. Let me show you how much I love you." And, she doesn't mean to think this, let me show you how to be a man. She quickly hugs his arm, smiles at him. "I've even got a plan."

Robie watches her as though she's something he hasn't quite seen before. The wind ruffles her hair. She's smiling to herself. The bridge slopes down into Brooklyn. They have to descend some stairs and walk back several blocks to find the River Café. The parking lot is almost empty. They stand a few minutes looking out over the water. Kathy points up to the high arching span of the bridge. "Right up there," she says, laughing, "they ought to put a plaque."

He impulsively hugs her, thinking, She's amazing, what an amazing creature. . . .

"You keep on the glasses," Kathy says. "Nobody knows me. Besides, you look good. . . . I'd think about doing it with you."

They go inside the restaurant and ask for a table in the corner; it seems the most secluded.

"Two brandies, that RSVP stuff," Kathy tells the unsmiling waiter.

"Sorry . . . oh, Remy Martin. VSOP," he corrects her.

Robert reaches across the table and holds her hands in his. Stretching out his arms until he can secretly stroke her breasts. They smile at each other. She pulls his hands more against her. "I can't get enough," he says, wondering if he's gone over some kind of edge. Technically, clinically? Or maybe his reactions are the most normal thing in his life. If he can have a phenomenal woman like this, maybe the sick thing would be to let it go. "Alright, go ahead"—his voice hesitates—"tell me the plan."

"Let's get the booze," she says.

"That was quite a surprise. On the bridge."

"It was . . . really great. Yeah, it was. Try it again on the way back."

"I'll have to take a cab up to the train."

"Robie, lighten up. It was a joke."

"Sorry."

"We'll do it here."

"Another joke?"

"You never know. . . . Do you?"

He shrugs. "Sometimes I don't."

The brandies come, and Kathy says, "A toast. To us, darling."

They touch glasses and sip the gently burning liquor.

"Ohhh, that's nice," Kathy says, "just the way I feel now."

"Seems more like straight Kentucky bourbon," Robert says. "You, I mean."

"Really? No, this is classier. I feel like this."

"Alright, tell me."

"We're doing it the hard way?"

"Well . . . you mean . . . Yes, I think it adds up better that way. Go on."

"Well, like you said, you see a lot of different stories in the papers. And one thing they do is go to somebody's house. At first, this seems crazy. But then you think about the other ways. Following somebody around, trying to catch them by surprise. What you were talking about, basically. Think about the problems. You can't be sure when the person will be somewhere. And you can't be sure who else might show up. So why not go where the person always is? Alone, thinking about the checkbook or something. You knock on the door, and say, Hi, I'm from down the street; can I come in, talk a minute? And that's all you need."

Robert listens to the tone as much as to the words. The very casual, very comfortable tone. Like she's talking about the weather or going on a trip somewhere. Yeah, she's right, she can handle it. He's impressed. Then relieved. Then apprehensive. The feelings going around in him.

"You can do this?" he says, not sure what to say.

"I told you already. And the thing is, you can always pull back. Abort, they say. You just have to be cool, see if the conditions are right. Otherwise, you don't go through with it. You quietly retreat and nobody knows anything."

"Maybe try again."

Kathy smiles. "There you go."

"And me?" Robert tries to appear ready for anything, but he's thinking about the word she used. A token. He liked the sound of that.

"You're the alibi. That way you don't have to be there. I mean, it's going to be harder for you than for me. But you're still a part of the deal."

She sips some more. Her face becomes more serious.

"I have to have that, Robie. Not because I couldn't take the risk by myself. I damned well could. But you have to do something for me, too. Otherwise, I don't want . . ."

She stares at him, sort of sadly, he thinks. It's rare she seems vulnerable. She does now. Letting him feel how important this is to her.

"No problem," Robert says. "*Whatever* you say." He squeezes her hand. "Tell me the rest." He smiles, trying to lighten the mood. "You've done your homework, I can tell."

"Alibi means you see me somewhere else. Say you tell the people in the office you have to go out for a walk, clear your mind. You just happen to see this woman you know on sight. Certain time, certain corner. Maybe we wave. No doubt in your mind it's her. Me. We'll run through it one day. But, hey, there's no reason it ever comes to an alibi. If everything goes right, it's just a mystery. You come home from work and . . . Well, that's what you have to be prepared for."

Robert finishes his glass. Thinks over what she's said. Tries to.

"The only other thing I need," Kathy says, "is a day when she's home. She take personal days? Bad periods?"

He nods. "Often she does. They're not that bad. But she figures she deserves a day—"

"When's the next one?"

Robert pauses, looking at the seriousness in Kathy's face.

She's thinking so fast, moving so fast. *When's the next one?* That's good. "Well, two weeks ago or so. . . . About ten days, I guess."

"Well, lover? What do you think?"

Robert glances uneasily about the room. It's all so real when Kathy talks about it. And so immediate. Hell, this is countdown. This is saying Anne's got ten days left. . . .

"You can just walk up to the house?" he asks. "Disguised or what?"

"It's typical suburban, right? Oh, I'll go up and take a look." She's sorry she never told him she was there. But this isn't a good moment either. "The houses aren't that close together, right? And who's looking? . . . Yes, Robie, I'd be disguised." She wonders if that's why she cut her hair short, because she always knew she'd end up wearing a wig, for one reason or another.

"You've thought of everything. I'm so impressed. . . . Really, it's amazing—"

"Stop, Robie. 'What do you think' means, *yes* or *no?*"

"Yes, absolutely. No question."

He grabs her hands, lifts them to his mouth, kisses her several times. Yes, he thinks, the best partner a man could possibly have. Everything to the limit. I won't even be there, I'll be miles away. God, I'm not sure I could've done it the other way. But this, this is perfect.

Kathy feels his lips on her fingers. Sees the way his head is bowed in front of her. The dream was getting away, at least she was frightened it was. But now, she thinks, I can make it happen, you just have to fight. A great day, that's what I figured.

"She's not suspicious, right?"

"No," Robert says. "I'm sure of it."

"Then there's no problem."

She slips down low on the seat, pushes a shoeless toe into his groin. "I don't know," she says, smiling, "this kind of talk does make a person horny, doesn't it?"

Robert kisses her hand some more, says in a joking way, "Don't. Please. We'll get arrested. I have—"

"Oh, I'm just talking. Relax. I won't do anything, even if you beg. . . . Well, maybe if you beg *real nice*."

"I don't know. . . . Horny? Maybe it does. You get me flying, I know that. I'm tingling all over, whatever the reason is. I'm surprised I know my name. . . . What is it, by the way?"

They laugh, all four hands in a writhing ball.

"It's amazing," Kathy says. "We're sitting here talking about doing away with you-know-who and I'm thinking about fucking on the table. . . . No! It's too late. You had your chance. Don't beg."

"Please."

"Oh, alright."

They laugh more loudly.

"Seriously, Kathy, it would be an honor to beg you." Robert looks puzzled. "Does that make sense?"

"Yes," she nods, "it's very sweet. Thank you."

"We'll get a cab back to the city," Robert says, "and I'll beg you all the way in." He raises a hand, signals the waiter. "I've got a wish list already."

"How many wishes?"

"Just three or four main ones."

"I'll try to hold out. . . . At least out of the parking lot."

They're laughing when the thin waiter comes over. He gives them a prim stare of reprimand. Kathy eases on her sunglasses, gives him a fuck-you smile.

PART

Chapter 28

Anne faces a wall in the firm's cafeteria, sitting alone, eating in an absentminded way.

Stan, a young attorney in the firm, is walking toward the serving line. He stops and watches her for a moment. Something very intent, even grim, about her. He hesitates to interrupt her, almost doesn't. A nice-looking woman, pleasant, smart, he thinks, probably a good body but not exactly Miss Conviviality.

Oh, well, he decides, putting on a big smile. He walks over and says, "Anne, hi. How's everything?"

She looks up with a blank expression. "Ohhh . . . Stan. Fine."

"Can I sit down a moment?"

"Certainly . . . of course."

Stan sits facing her. "You probably don't even remember . . . but I thought I'd tell you something."

"Yes?"

"Couple months ago. You were in here with one of the CPAs. A bunch of us were talking about this case, a burglary, guy got shot. Remember any of this?"

"I remember very well."

"Oh. Well, I remember it bothered you. So I can give you some good news. The whole thing got settled. Case just evaporated, actually. Happy?"

She stares at him. Stan doesn't get the feeling she's overjoyed to hear all this.

"Well, thank you, Stan," she says slowly. "Thanks for telling me."

Stan nods. "You do remember, right?"

She seems to snap a little. "Stan, I told you I recall the case precisely. It was offensive that you . . . that we would be involved in something like that."

Stan shrugs uneasily. "Well, people have a right to good counsel."

Anne puts down her fork. Stan watches this with a twinge of apprehension. "The man in the yard was a professional burglar," she says in a low but stern voice. "You knew that. He was not drunk. He was not lost. He was there to break into the house and steal. I don't pretend to know what proper punishment is. But the whole point of the legal system is to get the facts on the table. At least to try to."

Stan smiles. "Not if you're guilty."

Anne stops herself from responding. She picks up her coffee with both hands, takes her time sipping. Slow things down, stay calm.

Stan's just trying to be nice, she thinks. Edd took care of it, apparently—*he* was just trying to be nice. *Everybody* is trying to be nice. I'm so wound up, I have to be careful. Fake it, lady. Smile. Who cares about a damned burglar and the rest of it? Well, damn, I can't very well say what I really care about. Oh, Stan, by the way, I think my husband's planning to leave me. . . . Maybe something much worse. God, it hurts just to think that.

She gasps. Holds the cup away from her lips. "Still hot," she lies, trying to smile.

"Right," Stan says, looking uncomfortable. "Anyway, I just thought you would want to know." He stands up. "Well, I'll be—"

He glances across the room, sees Edd Lawrence walk in. Edd scans the room, sees them and comes right over. "Well, still here," he says to Anne. "Good, I'll join you. . . . Hi," he adds, turning to Stan.

Anne looks up at them. "Stan here was just saying that the burglar's suit has evaporated. That the word, Stan?"

"Is that so?" Edd exclaims. "I remember it."

"You do?" Stan says, surprised. "February . . . yes, I think it was—"

"Sure," Edd says. "Anne said it was a silly suit."

"I said it was disgusting," Anne corrects him. "I meant evil. Now, I wonder why I thought that. . . ." Now, she thinks, that I know a lot more about the subject.

Stan stares down at Anne. "Well . . ." He starts to walk away but doesn't. *"Now you wonder why?* I'm sorry?"

"You boys play your little games," Anne says, looking down. "And then you're surprised that people hate lawyers."

"Anne, really."

Anne is seeing Robert's face when she says, "It's just wrong, that's all. A man's home is his castle. And a woman's, too, I would hope." She pushes the tray back and stands up. Edd is watching her with his passive face, but she can feel his mind whirring. Anne confronts Stan. "We have to be responsible. Is that too much to ask? Life isn't a game, you know. I'm sorry, Edd, I have to get back to work."

"I'm sorry, too," Edd says.

Stan's face moves from one expression to another. Geez, I was just trying to be nice. And look what I get. What is going on here? I didn't know accountants got so crazy.

Anne makes a little wave, smiling some, trying to end on a lighter note. "Thanks, Stan. Well, I'll be going."

"You're welcome," he says, the words sounding ironic.

Anne starts across the room. Edd watches her, then sees Stan's confusion. "Interesting woman," Edd says.

Like that explains *anything*, Stan thinks. "Oh, yeah," he says vaguely. "Bye." Sorry he ever came over to talk to her.

•••

Anne settles at her desk, tries to concentrate on the numbers. . . . God, I feel like I'm on fire or something. *I can't do it now,* Robert says, and I think he's talking about divorce. No, no; now I don't think that's right. If it was divorce, he'd talk to me about it. He doesn't talk, so it's got to be something worse. Something unspeakable . . . as it were. And there's something in the tone of his voice, something hushed and conspiratorial. *We have to make sure everything's just right,* he says. What, for leaving me? I just assumed that's what he meant. But what would have to be *right?*

Every time I listen, I hear it in a darker way. Oh, I don't know what to think anymore. I don't know how to think about any of this. I mean, how do you? You have to be a cop or something like that. What was it, four or five years ago, Robert and I were joking, *You know, we're both worth a lot more dead than alive. Haha.* . . . Is that it?

She remembers the man who sold her the recording device. Sure, he'd know how to think about this. Everyday stuff. Maybe I should pick a lawyer out of the phone book, talk to him. Or go to the police. But they might just laugh. Well, lady, you want to press charges? What?! Everything's so inconclusive. All I've got's a half dozen sentences. That last time, they really start to talk and her mother calls! Call waiting. Now there's an old lady somewhere I don't even know and I hate her.

So who can I talk to? Maybe call up Mom, say, Remember your favorite son-in-law? Well, he might be . . . I couldn't speak the words.

I feel like such a lunatic just thinking about this, for suspecting that Robert could actually . . . Oh, I must be a lunatic. Yes, definitely. I've got this on my mind every other minute. So I'm a lunatic *for* thinking it. Or thinking it will *make* me a lunatic. Either way, I end up in the same spot. They get you in a padded room and people peek in the little window and you never get out. Sorry, lady, you thought crazy thoughts. Case closed, door locked.

Anne remembers that for several minutes before lunch she felt analytical, objective. Here's a puzzle, try to solve it, she told herself. Turn the pieces around until they make sense. She liked this feeling. It's the feeling she brings to her work, to solving the tax problems of her clients. But the feeling didn't last long. She tries to bring it back now. There's just a jumble of thoughts and in back of them a mist of fear.

She sits back violently, as if she can jolt these thoughts from her mind.

She looks up and sees Edd leaning in the door. He's smiling in his neutral way. She wonders if he saw her jump back like that. Yes, he must have.

He moves inside the office, stands there looking at her. "Anne . . . I'm sorry. I'm not sure how to say this. You seem very tense the last week or so."

Anne shrugs. "Oh, well . . . work's piling up on me. You know how it is."

She glances back and forth from the computer screen to Edd, wondering what he suspects, wondering if her behavior has changed in such an obvious way. She smiles, tries to appear very calm.

"Right," he says. "I know how it is." He hesitates, then adds, "Well, if there's anything I can do. . . ."

She looks at him more directly. Maybe Edd could help, she thinks. He's got a shrewd, even-tempered way of looking at problems. He'd probably know exactly what to do. I really wish I could trust him.

Edd watches her. Smiling some. Not much of a smile, but this, she thinks, is a man who hardly smiles at all. "If I can be of any help," he says, "you tell me."

"Yes, alright, Edd. I will."

He seems reluctant to leave. He looks out the window, then back at Anne. "I don't like seeing you upset. . . . I'd like to be able to help."

I wish you could, Anne thinks. I wish somebody could. She hesitates a moment, trying to think of some way to test him. "What do you think it is, Edd?"

"Well, I'm not sure, of course. . . . Maybe something at home. Anne, I really like you. I . . ."

Then she understands. He's making some kind of pass. She blinks, trying to think fast. "Edd, I like you, too. So let me be frank. There's nothing wrong at home. And I think you're a little out of line here." She hopes she hit just the right tone of seriousness. Let him think she's annoyed.

Edd stiffens, backs up a step. "I'm sorry. I didn't mean . . . to offend you. Well, if I can . . . Whatever it is, if I can help, you tell me. Promise?"

"Of course, Edd. Thank you."

He retreats into the hall. Anne shaking her head in surprise. Her heart pounding so she notices it. What'd he have in mind, she wonders. Things aren't right at home, so we jump in the sack? What would that be like? Dear God. Is this what happened to Robert? Somebody says, If things aren't right at home, maybe I can help. . . .

Nothing's what it was, Anne thinks, everything's gotten so sleazy I can't recognize it. Funny, Edd could probably help. I was seeing us as a team for a minute. Solving this together. Maybe figuring out how I should defend myself, if it comes to that. I thought I needed an ally. Now I don't think so. I'm all alone in this.

She grimaces, feeling proud and terrified in the same instant.

Robert, Robert. What has happened to you? To us? What

are you doing? I can't make sense of anything anymore.

She stares finally at the screen. Amounts of money spent for capital improvements, warehousing, executive bonuses, interstate transport. What is all this? she wonders. Does it mean *anything?* My husband's planning to kill me—*there*, I said it! Yes, yes, I really do think that's what is happening. Now *that* means something.

But I'm not even sure about that. *Maybe* he is. How do I figure this out? Robert, dear husband, could you possibly do such a thing? You're thinking of what—a gun, a knife, some arsenic?

She feels a sharp pain all the way down her right side.

"Oh, Jesus. . . . Look, I'm doing it for him."

She breathes as deeply as she can, trying to ease the pain.

She cannot imagine Robert doing this thing. Not to her, not face to face. "But," she hisses at herself, "*say* he does. How's he . . . ?" The first image she has is of a deserted road, an isolated spot. He wants to go to a great restaurant but it's over in Connecticut somewhere. "Five star, Anne, just an hour away." Then there's some kind of accident. Or he wants to take a little trip. Anyplace I'm not familiar with, really, then he . . . *they* . . . can set up something.

She smiles. If Robert mentions a trip now, I think I'd jump out of the chair. . . . No, I'd let him set it up, then change it all at the last minute, see if he objects.

That's the only thing she feels sure of, that something unusual will happen. Then she'll know. . . . No, she won't know. She'll be twice as tense, watching, waiting, trying to see this thing coming, whatever it is, before it's on top of her.

She shivers all over her chest, going back again to the question that most intrigues her: Could Robert actually think of such a thing, plan it, do it? No, no, no, Anne wants to cry out. No, it has to be this woman, this terrible person he's somehow gotten involved with. It's all her idea. Robert could grow tired of her, of course. But could he *hurt* her? No, it was unthinkable.

Anne realizes she's shaking all over, visibly trembling. She stands up decisively, stretches, tries to quiet herself. "Get a grip, lady." I've got to think clearly. It's the only hope I've got.

•••

At 4:15 Anne is in her boss's office, getting more orders, basically. Anne starts to leave, then says: "Estelle, I want you to know something."

"Yes, Anne?"

"I think I was more qualified for that promotion than the person you chose."

"Well, Anne," Estelle says, looking at Anne in a smug way, "I'm sure I know what's best for this company," Still, there's some confusion there, too. Her eyes narrow. What's got into Anne?

"I just want to be on record," Anne says, thinking, Hey, what's this office nonsense when your husband might be trying to kill you? "I want to be on record, that's all. Perhaps you will at some point review the performance of the individuals involved. . . ."

Anne lets it hang in the air. Estelle stares. What in the world?

Chapter 29

Robert leaves his office at 1:15 and goes down to 42nd Street and walks west toward Grand Central. He lights a small cigar and puffs it in an obvious way. He crosses Park and continues on, staying on the south sidewalk. Trying to seem lost in his worries about a big story, hardly aware of the people around him. But he can't resist glancing ahead. She'll be there, somewhere, suddenly, coming from Fifth.

He almost expects her to be larger than everyone else, to be glowing, to stand out somehow. He sees her in his mind as floating toward him, smiling, naked, her arms outstretched.

He doesn't see her until she's thirty feet away. A woman of ordinary size, larger people all around her. The other people moving away from him and toward him in a clumsy choreography that tends not to feature Kathy but to diminish and hide her. The close-cut black hair makes her seem even smaller than when he first met her.

She's staring straight ahead. Not looking for him at all. Or doing a better job of pretending than he is. At the last second she sees him and says, "Oh . . . Mr. Saunders . . . how are you?"

"Oh, fine . . . Kathy, isn't it?"

She smiles only fleetingly. "Yes, that's right. Well, duty calls. Bye."

And she's gone. And he almost turns around to call after her. Please, stop—hug me, kiss me, let me feel you. No, he tells himself sharply, keep walking. He crosses Madison and then Fifth. He stands on the steps in front of the big library. Smoking the rest of his cigar, staring up at the warm blue sky. Solving that big story. Thinking actually about how obsessed he is with this woman, how in love he is. Thinking what a good actor she is. Thinking of the word *rehearsal*, what Kathy calls this. "Today is just for me," she said. "On the actual day you'll leave more tracks. Tell your secretary you're going out to think, and so on." *Rehearse* . . . funny, I never noticed the word *hearse* in there before; are they really spelled the same? I'll have to look that up. He grins uncomfortably. Then he comes down the steps and crosses in front of the library and heads back on East 41st. In seven minutes he reaches Third, turns left and goes into the lobby of his building.

He comes back to his office, his desk, sits down at what used to be his favorite spot in the whole world. Now that's wherever she is. He feels the tingle of anxiety along his arms, the worry, the fear. But at the moment they are faint and far away. Not a problem, he tells himself.

I'm fine, he thinks. Everything's fine.

He has the sense of falling into a dark pool. But it's not scary, it's pleasant. A dark, tropical pool perhaps. Everything is warm and sensuous. The only texture is the way her skin feels. Her voice is the only sound he hears. The only smell is Kathy's smell. . . .

"Mr. Saunders? . . . Hello?"

"Oh, Wilson . . . I'm sorry." He focuses on the young reporter in front of his desk. "What?"

"You said we'd discuss the Board of Ed story."

"Thieves and idiots." Kathy, so real a moment before, fades.

"I'm sorry?"

"My opinion, not the paper's. Pull up a chair. But I want you to bear down on this crew. We've got to have better schools."

"Oh, yes, sir."

"Feet to the fire, that kind of thing."

"I'd like that." He leans eagerly toward Robert, eager for editorial guidance.

Yeah, this is definitely what I'm good at, Robert thinks. And maybe nothing else. The Peter Principle. Everybody finally reaches the level where they're incompetent. Where they're bound to fail. This thing with Anne, maybe that's the level I shouldn't try for. Kathy thinks she can just bop up there on the train, stop by to commit a . . . murder, and waltz right back. "Who's to know?" she says. "Takes less than ninety minutes. A long lunch hour. You can say you saw me somewhere in there, so it can't be me. And the day before, the day after, I'll stop in shops around here, talk to people. Weeks later you think anybody can be sure which day it was?" Jesus, the audacity. Woman's something. If anybody can do it, it's her. . . .

"Mr. Saunders?"

"Yeah?" He focuses on the reporter again. "Just thinking it over. . . . Your story."

God, I'd give anything to see her today. Have her right here on this desk, legs apart, drawing the skirt up an inch at a time. Slooowwww. No, faster, I have to see it. Every beautiful black hair. . . .

"Mr. Saunders . . . if this isn't a good time?"

Robert snaps at him. "It's a *great* time. Let me think."

"You're sure?"

"I am positive." He lets Kathy fade again, reluctantly, just as she lifts the skirt, then the sheer slip, leaning away from him. He feels a rush through his body, lust, anger, panic. He isn't faking his sudden ardor. "Damn it, Wilson, just burn them! The biggest per capita budget in the universe, and the worst results. Sherman through Georgia—be that."

"What is Sherman through Georgia?"

"Jesus! Are you serious? They teach anything in school anymore?"

"I beg your pardon."

"Well, you can't have it. . . ."

Robert wants to stand up, storm around some. But he realizes he's got an erection and better stay seated. This dope graduated from college and J school and he doesn't know what Sherman through Georgia is. Are things really that bad? Robert feels old. Horny beyond belief and old.

His heart is pounding. Oh, just do it, Kathy. This world's not that big a deal; people getting dumber by the month. If I can't have you, fuck it. He glowers at the reporter.

"Wilson, feet to the fire, okay? I should've stopped when I was ahead. If they all call up here bitching and moaning, then you did a good job. Got it?"

"Yes, sir. . . . Uh, what will you tell them?"

"Only one thing to tell them, Wilson. . . . There's this loose cannon on the paper. Guy's wild. I can't control him. You, Wilson. Get to work."

The guy retreats in delighted panic. Robert sighs, closes his eyes, sees Kathy's smile.

Chapter 30

Anne is in her nightgown, standing in front of the basin, brushing her teeth. Looking at herself now and then in the mirror. Does she look the same? She checks her eyes, whether she can see white above and below the pupils. A sure sign of stress, she's read this. She squints, then relaxes, trying not to fake the results. No, no white. So she's all right? She looks normal? Does this mean people can't tell that she's a lunatic?

She hears Robert moving around in the bedroom, mumbling, looking for something maybe?

Who is he, anyway? This really nice sweet husband she's lucky to have? This demented adulterous killer? How does she find out, except to find out? That is, to let things unfold until she knows for sure. Curiosity, this intense curiosity, fills her like a thin nausea.

I've got to know, she thinks. And then she thinks, And I've got to be ready. And what's that mean? A gun, some Mace, a nice knitting needle? What do I know? It means *be ready*. They'll do it somewhere else? No, maybe here. More and more, she thinks, Why not here? Anything can happen inside a house, and nobody can know.

She looks closely at her hair. Not a strong color, sort of brown-blond. Mousy, people say mousy. I hate that. I never saw a mouse this color. So what's it mean? They're talking about me? I'm a mouse? Damn it, I don't see that. I'm a well-mannered, well-bred, well-educated person. Where's mousy get into this?

Well, I like the way it's cut. Little swing on the sides there, little bounce. And look at those shoulders. Strong-looking, I think. Somebody calls me mousy, they better have stronger shoulders. Hey, lady, how'd you like a rap in the mouth?

She grins self-consciously through the foam of the toothpaste. Who am I kidding?

Robert is suddenly behind her. Staring at her in the mirror. Smiling, well, almost. He's got his blue pajama shirt on. He holds her shoulders firmly, leans closer and kisses her neck. Now he's licking her bare skin.

She spits out the toothpaste, then palms some water up to her mouth. Aware when she bends that Robert is pressing his hips against her. Not his hips, actually, his erection. His hands are now around her, squeezing her breasts through the silk of the nightgown. Roughly, but it's pleasurable.

"Uuuhhhmmmmm," he says in her ear. Smiling more now, looking her in the eye, in the mirror. "You feel good."

His tongue is in her ear. She flinches and cringes. Then she realizes his hands are on her thighs, lifting the nightgown. Getting it up to her waist. One hand sliding around to the front of her. Robert bending his knees, butting his erection up under her ass.

Look at him, she thinks. Wilder and wilder. Just walks in and starts at it. Where's he learned this? And what's it *mean?* Does he love me? Does he even *want* me? Is this acting, so

I won't suspect anything? She feels curiously empty. Dead? she wonders. Dead already?

To her surprise, this thought doesn't make her angry. *Empty . . . dead . . .* this sense of herself is somehow liberating. I'm dead? Then what the hell? What the bloody hell?

She stands on her tiptoes, leaning over on the basin, helping him get inside her. Hell, she's already wet. Ahh, there, he eases up into her vagina, out and more strongly back in, almost lifting her off the tile floor.

Anne makes herself look at the mirror, and stare into his eyes. Wanting to scream, Great, dear husband . . . do it a long time, just like this. Then thinking that if she said this *with feeling*, she'd start crying. Yes, she would, she's sure of it. Better to be cold, empty . . . and free.

She juts her ass out toward him, pushing back at his thrusts. She reaches back for his hands, presses the right one over her breasts, the left one on her belly. He's a large man, he seems to be all over her, in her and around her. His big left hand pushing in hard on her belly—he knows she likes this. Then the little finger hooks around under the pubic bone, and she gasps.

She stares at his mouth, realizes he's kissing her neck back and forth, licking her and slobbering all over. She can see his spit glistening on her skin.

What is it, Robert, what's going on?—she thinks as she twists in his grip. Here, sweetie, kiss my toothpaste mouth. I'm dead. There's no rules.

He finally sees she's turned and his full mouth is on her lips and his tongue goes inside her mouth and then he seems to be licking the toothpaste off her. Why wasn't it always like this, Robert? Why'd you have to learn from somebody else?

If, she almost screams in his eager mouth, you did. If that's what has happened.

The tension of not knowing, of not being sure of anything, seems to build in her along with the sexual tension. Maybe, she thinks, it's the main thing. Her muscles vibrate with the tension of *I want to know!* She seems to tighten and tighten, faster than she can remember it ever happening before. *God Almighty ooohhhh Robert sweetheart what's happened to us?*

•••

She lies awake next to Robert, hearing his breathing fill the dark room. Is that the sign? she wonders. That he just grabbed me by the sink? It never happened like that before. What!—he wanted one last quickie before he injects me with something in the middle of the night? She shudders.

Yes, she thinks, it might be . . . She worries she won't be able to sleep, that she'll have to lie awake all night, waiting. Oh, God. I'm getting to be like those gunslingers in westerns. A twig snaps and my eyes jump open. This is no way to live.

Then she thinks again of what Robert did. . . . No, it's not a sign, she decides. It's part of the whole pattern. He keeps getting more reckless, that's all. Funny thing, I like it. If I didn't have the messages on the machine, I might be able to say, Oh, isn't this wonderful, my husband's more crazy about me than ever! I am so lucky.

But I do. . . .

He loves somebody else. Something is going to happen. Dear God, give me the strength. Truth is, I'm smarter than Robert. The cunning's there, I just have to sharpen it. But the strength, the bravery, that's what I'm going to need. *Me brave?* Oh, it gets better all the time.

How am I going to get any sleep? I'm so wound up, it's killing me. "Hey, Robert," she says softly, knowing he won't hear her, "you want to do it again?"

There, *he*'s tossing a little. He can't sleep either. Not peacefully. A certain intensity has crept into everything he does. That's how I know things are bad.

Anne thinks back over the last few weeks. Robert really hasn't complained much about work. Maybe in a perfunctory way, maybe as an excuse for being late, but not really. Money's okay. No medical problems. Really, what's he got to be tense about? But he is, he really is. But all this time he's doing this offhand act. Aw shucks, just us happily marrieds having a good old time.

Anne, one theory is he's planning something horrible. Give me another theory. . . .

She thinks fleetingly of one she tried to hold on to, that Robert has this girlfriend who's giving him a hard time. She's a mistake, he wants to get rid of her. What a lovely theory. But then Anne crashes again into the first message when he said, *Miss you,* and then the second one when they talked a minute. The feeling's very calm, soft, intimate. No, this Kathy is *not* giving him a hard time. Not at all. . . .

Anne shudders all over, trying to let the anxiety out of her body. Then she feels anger rise in its place. Damn it, Anne, there aren't any other theories. There's only one.

She hears Robert snoring faintly. She realizes her eyes are wide open, staring up into the dark room.

Chapter 31

"This little bar," Kathy says. "It's where we had our second date. It was the first time you touched me."

"Boy, what that started," Robert says, trying to sound upbeat. He sips some of the straight bourbon on ice he's got.

"I can tell you the date. February 16th."

"Sometimes you don't seem very sentimental. Then you do."

"I actually am. It's more fun that way. If you keep up your end, I'll be Mrs. Mush."

Robert grins, a little uneasily, glancing around. "I'm sorry we don't have more time."

"I know, I *know*," she laughs. "But how, you want to know, do you get laid?"

"Well . . ."

"Can't get enough, huh?"

"I can't."

"Music, sweet music. Well, there *is* a phone booth back there."

"And?"

"And *anything*. . . . I'll sit, you'll *stand up*."

"Oh, that took my breath away."

She strokes his hands. Gives him a look that turns his skin crimson.

"Kathy, Kathy, wait a minute. While I can still think at all. . . ."

"Alright, what?"

"Alright, let's say she stays home on the 12th. It's go?"

"You tell me."

Kathy watches him with a slight frown on her face. She tilts her head slightly, waiting, trying to smile, trying not to show disappointment.

"I just have to see this clearly," Robert says. "I mean, that you can actually pull this off. Maybe there's no cab when you need it. Or maybe you can't get away from the office. It's a Wednesday or Thursday, for sure."

"If I can't, I can't. I told you, I go along the road until I have to turn back. Or I'm sure and I go ahead."

"Well," Robert muses, "I suppose something could be done on a weekend."

"Yes. But the more I thought about it, the more I liked a workday. It's just not what anyone would expect. And I really know I can leave a lot of false clues, all over the place, without that much trouble. I'm not even going to tell you everything. You don't need to know."

"Really?"

"First anniversary. I'll tell you then."

Robert stares at her, always amazed at how far ahead she thinks. He feels as if he's stumbling and lurching from one day to the next.

"Well, we've got the alibi, the codes, everything is clear. . . ." He hesitates.

"Damn it, Robie. . . . Yes or no? Stay or go?"

"What?"

They rub each other's hands, stare for a moment.

"Robie," she sighs. "Make a decision and stick with it. . . . Be a man."

He looks at her, sees a sadness in her face that he hates. He knows he's letting her down, not doing his half, not being as strong as she is. It torments him. "You're right," he says with utter sincerity. "You are 100 percent right. I love you, Kathy Becker, that's all that matters. You're the most wonderful miracle I can imagine."

"That's nice." Now she's smiling again. She sits forward suddenly, standing partway, and kisses him on his mouth. Her hands caress his head and as she sits back, one hand presses down his chest and fleetingly touches his pants.

"Damn," he says, angry with himself. "I'm the one who figured all the pros and cons. I got us here. . . . I'm sorry. No more bullshit. And the truth is, I have complete confidence in you. Hell," he laughs, "you ever think about being a spy or a Green Beret, something like that?"

"Ohhh, now you're making me horny. . . . Only, darling, if you were the prize."

"Mrs. Mush, huh? Sometimes you say the sweetest things." He takes a loosely folded blue handkerchief out of his jacket pocket. Something solid about seven inches long wrapped inside. "What you asked . . ."

She takes the handkerchief and slips it in her purse. "Well," she says, smiling again, "I am probably the sweetest girl you know."

"It's true."

"You really want to get in that phone booth, don't you?"

"No. . . . I was just pointing out the truth."

She jerks his arms out straight, so his fists press into her breasts. "I want to," she says sternly. "Please don't say no."

"Well, if you're going to twist my arm."

"That's not all."

She's laughing as she stands up by the table and pulls him up, too.

PART

Chapter 32

Anne wakes up a few minutes after seven. She stares with one eye at the light coming through the east window. She shifts her attention to the body behind her. Robert's breathing is low and smooth.

She focuses on her body. She doesn't feel that good. Tense and on edge. She seems to wake up very fast. She has a sense that her mind is also on edge.

She flexes her left arm against her breasts. They're tender. She remembers the way Robert hugged her the night before, as they were saying good night. He dropped his arm across her chest and when she winced, he said, "Oh, sorry. You're sensitive. You having your period?"

Did he ever say anything like that before? She thinks he might have. But the way he put his arm down on her. . . . It seemed deliberate. As if he wanted to make her wince. So that then he would have a pretext for saying, "You having your period?"

And how did she answer? "It's about here." She thinks those were the words.

And what did he say? "Well, maybe you'll grab a sick day? Well, 'night, dear."

Grab a sick day? So casual. Then he drops it. He never said such a thing before, she's sure of that. The whole matter is so unpredictable, in lots of ways. Men learn to leave the subject alone. The fact is, she could never really know until the next day how she was going to feel. Robert knows that. Talking about a sick day is like talking about next week's weather. Not much point.

She knows she's on edge, probably thinking rashly and overreacting. Still, she has a powerful feeling of artifice, of furniture not being in the right place. Just what she's been watching for, tensely and carefully.

She slides slowly out of bed and goes into the bathroom. There she splashes water in her face, shakes her head, and decides, *Yes, I'll go with it.*

Fifteen minutes later she's dressed. Robert hasn't woken up yet. She goes and kneels down by the side of the bed. She studies his sleeping face for a minute. Then she shakes him gently.

" 'Morning."

He blinks, then his eyes open wide. "Anne . . . what?"

"Wake up, sleepyhead. Listen, I don't feel so hot. I'm going to pick up a few things at the drugstore. Maybe stop by the office. Then I'll take the day off."

Now Robert really stares at her. "Ohhhh . . . alright."

"You'll be gone when I get back." She leans and kisses his cheek. "Bye, sweetheart. Have a good day."

"Oh," he stammers, sitting up a little, "I'm sorry you're feeling bad."

"No big deal." She laughs briefly. "Me *too*." She stands up, staring at him, wondering, Is this how we say good-bye forever?

"Bye," Robert says. He waves vaguely.

She thinks there's something sad in his face? Or he just hates waking up?

"Bye, honey."

She walks slowly away from him and out into the hall. Not feeling any better than when she woke up. Perhaps a little worse, from moving so fast. She doesn't have a choice on this. She figures she has to get out of the house quickly, leave him alone.

As she goes out the front door, she thinks: Yet another squalid little trap. And despite herself, she feels disloyal. She feels . . . evil.

She starts up the car, shaking her head in disbelief at her own feelings. Disloyal? Well, we'll see who's disloyal. I just hope it is me. Me a little bit. Instead of him a whole lot. Please, God, that's what I want. You know what I mean. . . .

Anne drives slowly and by an indirect route to a large DrugCo store. I do need a few things, she thinks. No lie there.

When she gets out of the car, she studies the sky more carefully than before. Cloudy. And it looks like the kind of overcast that will stay around. The air feels cool and damp.

Who cares? I'll be snuggled up in bed, if I want. . . . *I care.* If it's not Robert and whatever is happening there, then it's cramps and sweating. And if that's not enough, what the hell, then we get this lousy kind of weather. I won't have one reliable thought the whole day.

Go slow, sister, she tells herself as she walks to the store. I'm giving you this advice free. Go slow.

She's wondering how she'll kill an hour. Already wishing she was back home and listening to the recorder, already dreading it.

She looks at her watch, calculates the train Robert's mostly likely to catch, when he'll leave the house, whether someone in Manhattan would still be home at that time or on the way to work.

Then she thinks, It's just a hunch, isn't it? An evil hunch.

Grab a sick day? Grab? Sort of slangy for Robert. The way somebody talks when they're trying to seem casual. When they're lying, that is.

She stays in the store a long time, walking up and down the aisles. They seem surprisingly bright and full of interesting objects. Why, look at that . . . they make a denture adhesive out of the glue in kelp!

Anne decides not to stop by the office. She's not sure she can handle routine chatter. Even this early there'll be people there. All the A types hunting ahead of the pack. . . .

She feels exquisitely keyed up. A painful state but somehow, she thinks, a valuable one. One she doesn't want to lose.

Her watch says 8:22. Robert's bound to be gone by this time. Still, what's the rush? Who wants bad news?

She works toward the checkout line to pay for the few items she has. As the cashier rings up the purchase, Anne glances out the big windows. It's raining, in a slow, mournful way that makes her think of funerals.

Yes, I'm supposed to be in one, aren't I? I'm supposed to be the victim here.

"Your change, *ma'am*."

Anne looks at the cashier, surprised. "Oh yes . . . of course. Thank you."

What did that boy say? "Victims are shit, ma'am." Yes, I think that was it. At the time, I was more upset by the word *ma'am* than what he said. *As* upset. Either way, that seems kind of funny now.

Anne puts the change away and walks back to her car. The rain splattering lightly on the windshield. A heavy drizzle. She starts the motor and the wipers. She stares out through the shiny windshield. Well, she thinks, I don't want to be a victim, not in any sense.

She drives slowly, taking a somewhat long way, back to her street. Then she goes faster, intending to keep on going if she sees Robert's car in the drive. Oh, I could have gone by the train station, checked the parking lot there, found his car. I've got to think ahead. . . . No, the drive's empty.

She pulls in, feeling awkward and conspicuous. She's not sure why. What the hell, I live here. No, I know why. This is when you check the trap, see what you caught. And you hope the trap's empty. . . . No, maybe not. Maybe I want to get this over with. . . .

She walks quickly through the light rain. Inside the door, she carefully throws the dead-bolt lock. Then, taking off her coat, she walks slowly about the house, wanting to make sure nothing is open, that no one could possibly surprise her.

She holds off until 9:01. Robert's always on the train by that time. Usually he's at his office.

She stands a moment at the top of the stairs leading to the basement. Holding the railing. Taking inventory of her body, to see which parts hurt, which parts are happily unaware she's kicking another egg downstream.

Oh, yes, I have to call the office. . . . Oh, hell, let's deal with this.

In another minute she's sitting by the stack of blankets. Everything quiet upstairs. She pushes the button marked PLAYBACK.

There's a hang-up. Somebody calling us? No, Robert hung up here. . . . "Oh, there you are. In the shower?"

"Ummm, yeah."

"Well, it looks like the day."

"Sick day?"

"Yes. Here all day, I'd think. Thought you ought to know right away. I'm still home. Anne went to the drugstore."

"Roger. Big 10-4, darling."

"Good luck."

"Don't worry. Oh, I'll leave a message about the walk, exact time. Figure maybe late lunch hour."

"Got it. Love you."

"Yours truly too."

Then clicks. Anne pushes STOP while she can still move. Snakebite must feel like this. A heavy paralysis that begins in the heart and widens.

She sits without moving, staring at the gray cement floor for a long time.

Chapter 33

Kathy decides to move as early as she can. She's on the 11:56, a blonde in a cheap tan raincoat and a pale blue scarf and reading glasses. Two fake moles on her chin and cheek, some darker makeup under her eyes, so she'll look tired and ordinary.

She sits by a window, turned sharply toward it. Watching the rain wash down the glass, the colorless buildings beyond. Great weather, she thinks. Couldn't be better. Everybody outside looking at the ground, people with their collars up. A soft light that makes everything look the same.

Feeling pretty good, Kathy thinks, considering. It's funny how Robie talks as if this is an adventure or something brave. No, it's just work. You want anything in life, you have to work for it. You wade through it. Like you have an abortion or a baby, or the doc wants to cut something out of you. It's just work. And then you go on living. But God knows you aren't proud of it. It's just something you have to do.

Dad, shit that he was, had that much right. "You want something, baby, work for it, then it's yours, fair and square." Some work's more complicated than others. But hell, I feel like there's almost nothing I couldn't do. Good old Keith, sitting in jail. Thanks, man.

Now and then Kathy scans the few people in the car. To see if anybody is watching her or if there's anyone who might be a threat. A cop type, maybe. Somebody who remembers details as a matter of routine. She figures that somebody like that is the only thing she has to worry about. That or seeing someone she knows. But there's not many of those, and they're working in Manhattan at this time. Who the hell goes to Westchester in the middle of the day? Nobody. It doesn't happen, she doesn't exist.

Kathy checks her watch. Less than ten minutes to the station. Find Robie's car and then it's show time.

She stares out the window some more. Feeling a little sad. Not because of what she's got to do but because she's doing more than Robie is. That's a weight on her. That really it was she who pushed the thing over the edge. Left to Robie, what was going to happen? She hates to think the words: maybe nothing.

Kathy winces.

Man, I'm making this thing happen. I see the rainbow slipping away and I know what I have to do. But why'd Robie let it slip? . . . Oh, the hell with it. I do this, and then we've got the rest of our lives together. The man I want, the life I want. It's right there. I just have to reach out and take it.

A house in Westchester. Robie and her padding around on weekends. Having some babies soon enough. All of it's in her mind, more real than the blurred world outside the window.

The conductor calls out, "Bronxville."

She opens her pocketbook and takes out a pair of cheap leather gloves, only a little darker than the color of her skin.

She waits until the train is stopped and people are moving off the train. Then she stands and walks off quickly, her head down. In a minute she's in the parking lot, almost sprinting through the steady rain toward Robie's car. It's almost exactly where she was seeing it in her head. She kneels by the left rear tire, reaches around behind the cold rubber, immediately finds the keys.

She starts up the car and drives along a route she has memorized in detail.

The thing is, Robie thinks what I'm doing is a lot more dangerous than it is. Still he lets me. But hell, I had to make sure he saw the worst of it. Had to make sure he really accepted it, that he could live with it. All right, at least we got that part settled.

Then she smiles to herself. Hell, I've got fall-back positions on top of fall-back positions. Good old New York, good state for killing people. Even if they actually got me, I'd be out in six or eight years. Miss Perfect Behavior. But it ain't never going to happen that way.

Kathy walks through it again. Alright, they grab me coming out of the house. That's five hundred to one, at best. So alright, I say, Gee, it was horrible! I just came up here to talk to this woman about her husband and me. Real friendly. But she couldn't handle it, went all to pieces! Attacked me with an ashtray, then a lamp. It was all I could do to get away from her. Lucky for me, I ran into the dining room, pulled out a drawer, got the first knife I saw. She comes running at me. I held up the knife, and she just about ran into it. I was completely shocked. Believe me, it was horrible! . . . Sounds good to me. So what've you got there, at worst manslaughter. Maybe even accidental death. Worst case, I walk in ten to thirty—months!

Kathy grins. He waits, of course. He visits me every week. Of course. Or he's got me to worry about. . . . Robie still can't figure why I wanted one of their knives. I'm not telling. Come on, Robie boy, think. . . .

That's it. Anything goes wrong, and I think they'll crack

it, I work a few things out with Robie, go straight to the cops, lay it on them, take the fall.

But if I'm out clean, there's no way they'll catch me. I'm not even here. I'm having a bad lunch on Sixth Avenue right now, and I need to walk in the rain to clear my head. I call in, then I go over to the Public Library and then Bryant Park, hang around some. Then I pass Robert Saunders on the way back. Hi, Mr. Saunders!

Kathy remembers all the little stops she made yesterday. Stops she'll make tomorrow, also. People who'll say, "Yeah, she was in my place. Sure, around lunch, I'm sure of that much."

Hell, a week later, who remembers which day anything happened? And even worst case, the cops don't figure anything out for days, but probably weeks. Everything's muddled and forgotten by then. Beyond a reasonable doubt, for sure. And nobody in all of Westchester can ID me anyway.

All I have to do is drive carefully and don't get in any wrecks on this nice rainy day. And we're coasting downhill all the way home.

Kathy drives to a street that's perpendicular to Robie's street and stops forty yards from the corner. A street where cars routinely park along the curb. She sits a moment, checking her gloves, her pocketbook, the keys. Making sure everything is in order. Then from the pocketbook she takes a small fold-up umbrella and half opens it. As she does so, she stares down at the silver knife, making sure it's in its place.

Okay, girl, close the pocketbook, open the door, open the umbrella, get out and walk like it's just another day.

Chapter 34

Anne realizes she's hungry. All morning sitting, thinking, worrying, aching. She stares back toward the kitchen. She's afraid to fix food now. Never mind. She can't relax enough to eat. . . .

It's 12:19. The woman on the phone said, "Maybe late lunch hour."

Anne's in her dining room, positioned so she can look out at the front lawn, the front walk. The rain still falling through a gray mist. The light increasing as the sun moves to zenith. The day seems now to glow.

Anne feels sure that someone will come to the house. The idea is still in her head that two people might appear. Robert and someone else. She dreads this with all her being.

That he would do this is horrible. And what defense would she have against her own husband? What emotional defense?

She's not sure, but she thinks she'll just bolt out the back door, run to the nearest neighbor. Maybe jam the front door first, then flee. . . .

Stay just long enough to see that second person. That's the impossible task, to leave without seeing . . . *her*.

But maybe it'll be one person. One woman. Anne listened to the tape five times. The tone of voice, the words, the various meanings. And of course the words that made listening almost impossible. "Love you."

Each time she thinks these words, Anne feels herself start to tremble.

Damn, get steady. The point of the conversation seems to be that I'm home all day. Grabbing a sick day. That's what Robert called to tell that woman. *Her*.

Yes, obviously. But then Anne thinks, But maybe nobody will appear . . . and all of this is just fantasy. Some bizarre misunderstanding.

But I have to *find out*.

Yes, she accepts that. She's willing to play it out. But shouldn't she call for help, leave messages with people—*If I don't call back by three, send the cops*. Should she mail letters? Hide notes in places the cops will look? The same ideas she's played with for weeks. And they still don't sound right.

Maybe it's all her crazy imagination. "Well," she murmurs aloud, "the embarrassment won't be imaginary." She thought all morning of calling Edd at work, or one of the secretaries, or that young lawyer, Stan, or her mother or brother, or a friend, and leaving some sort of cryptic message. And every scenario she thought of ended in nothing happening and these people thinking she's crazy forever. She doesn't know enough. . . .

She especially wants to call Edd, trust him, bring him into this. But just the act of calling proves that she *knew*, that she was waiting. And what might it look like? she wonders. Something sleazy, absolutely. People would say, Oh, you and your *lover* plotted murder and revenge—confess! What lawyers could do with that. No, there's no way to call Edd.

No way to call anyone. She has to do it herself. Finally, Anne decides, she can trust only herself.

Funny thing, she thinks, I seem to want it that way.

Alright, the one person comes. *Her.* What then? She just walks in here and shoots me? Or she talks to me awhile first, explaining that this is necessary, because I'm obsolete and boring and not nearly pretty enough.

Damn it, this is my house. I know my way around. I know how the doors close and what locks. I can defend it.

Anne again scans the dining room, the living room, recalling which objects might be weapons, how she will maneuver or attack or run.

But there's really only one main thing. Kathy thinks I don't know she's coming. I do know. She's thinking she can surprise me. I'm thinking I can surprise her. Why not?

She definitely won't appear unless she believes I don't expect her. That much is logical, and that's about all that is.

Anne shivers from fear and tension. Her abdomen hurts. Anne tries to find something funny in all this. Well, she's going to be one surprised little bitch, if I'm right. . . .

Anne's face creases in a macabre smile. I just have to think of this as high-level negotiation and put some offers on the table she doesn't expect. Pretend she's from the IRS and that my sacred responsibility is to fuck her, as the boys at the office would say. Let's see. . . . Hey, the cops are upstairs. . . . No. Hey, the people across the street are watching the house—they're calling the cops right now. . . . Oh, Robert just called and said, Forget it, the deal's off. He loves me, you scum.

Anne starts crying, wishing it were true, facing the fact it's not. "Love you," the man said.

Yeah, *bitch!* Hey, I need some bagpipe music. We are going to war here. . . .

Wishing the bitch good luck as she's off to kill . . . me. . . .

Jesus God. Until that second I was hoping. Just kept making more hope. Where did I get it from? And now what? The adrenaline's up, then it's down. The pain comes, then it fades. I'm just numb. Empty. That's the thing. Even if they don't kill me, I'm dead anyway. Or dying. One of those insect things, you think it's alive, then you see it's just a husk. Locusts, I think. When I was a kid, I was always fascinated by those.

Anne peers out the window. There's *somebody* . . . Yes, a woman looking at the house. A woman alone! Here she comes through the bright rain. A pocketbook, a raincoat. If she's got a weapon, it's in the coat pockets or the pocketbook. Yes, she's doing it herself. Robert—you cad! Let's see. . . . Hey, not that pretty, after all. . . . Looks like a waitress at a bad coffee shop.

Anne's spirits rise. She walks quickly to the kitchen. She takes the receiver from the phone, wraps it in a towel and puts it in the back of an open drawer. She pushes the drawer shut. Can't have any distractions now.

Then she holds out her left hand and fills her palm with ground pepper, pressing the four fingers tightly down.

She drops the hand casually to her side, shakes any loose pepper to the floor.

"Just a thief," Anne mutters, "that's all you are. Think you can take my husband and now you want my life, too. You think you can take everything—"

The doorbell rings.

Anne rushes back to the front door, takes a huge deep breath, and unlocks the door.

The woman's there, staring at her through the glass storm door. Smiling in an inquiring way. "Hello? . . . Can I talk to you a moment?"

"Are you selling something?" Anne regards her in a bored way. Is this the voice on the recorder?

"Oh, no," the woman laughs easily, holding the umbrella out of the way so Anne can see how sincere she is. "We might move into this neighborhood. Down the street. I wanted to ask you how you like it here . . . if you wouldn't mind. Just take a minute. My name's Phyllis Bender. My husband works at IBM."

"Oh, well, of course," Anne says, unlocking the latch on the glass door. "A new neighbor, huh? Well, come in out of the rain."

"Thank you," the woman says.

Chapter 35

I'll never see her alive again. The thought gets into his head by eleven. Then he can't get rid of it. The more he tries not to think it, the more it's there.

Robert can't concentrate on the projects in the office. Stories, messages, meetings, it's all a blur and he's not sure which of it is real and which is something he should have done or intends to do later in the day. He starts trying to construct Kathy's timetable, what she'll be doing at each minute. He rummages in his desk for a train schedule. Let's see, if she leaves on this train, she'll reach Bronxville at this time, reach the house six minutes later, it'll all be over at this time. . . . Oh, God, I'll never see her again.

The big wall clock's at 11:54. It's all starting to happen. . . . He begins wondering if there's some way to call it off. Theoretically speaking. Anne's home, I can just pick up the phone, stop it. Just call her and say . . . what? Let's see. . . .

"Anne, this might be a big shock. Be calm. This woman I know is coming there to talk to you. Tell her to call me before she says one word. . . ."

"Anne, I have a terrible confession. I'm having an affair. Well, not an affair exactly. But this woman thinks it is and she's coming there to talk to you. Don't worry. I love you. All that matters is that you tell her, right at the door, that I called, and she has to call me immediately. . . ."

"Anne, this is Robert. I love you. Get out of the house immediately. Go out the back door. Go to the Griswolds' house. I'll call you there. . . ."

"Anne, this is Robert. Do not open the front door. Not for any reason. There's a crazy person loose in the neighborhood, it's on the news. I'm on my way. . . ."

The minute hand moves to sixteen minutes after twelve. He studies the timetable again. There's a 12:15. That's probably the one. She'll be in Bronxville at 12:45. At the house by 12:52. That's my deadline. . . .

He stares at the second hand. It seems to be whirling. Amazingly fast.

He thinks of the things he can say . . . editing the words . . . anticipating the things Anne will say—"What! . . . Oh, Robert, this is horrible. . . . How could you?"

"Never mind all that, Anne. Let's deal with the present." Yes, take command. . . . I like the crazy-person idea, but eventually she'll find out there's no crazy person, and I'll have to explain why Kathy was at the door. But I can save her for sure. If she lets Kathy in the house, God only knows. . . .

Hey, what about the cordless phone? I'll tell Anne to take it to the door, hand it out to the person at the door. Don't talk to her, Anne. Don't let her in. Make her stand back four feet. Put the phone out on the stoop. Yes, that's it. Alright, I'd have to tell her the truth, some of it, but at least I can stop everything. Then the truth'll be out. And we'll deal with that. Kathy can say, I'm here to talk things over. No mention of . . . anything else. Anne never has to know.

Oh, dear God, how did I ever get into this position? I mean, this is really crazy. I'm an accessory. . . . I do love Anne, that's the amazing thing. Maybe not as much as I love Kathy. But if you add everything up, it's not all that different. Maybe she'd have let me go. Why didn't I just ask her straight out? Damn it, Anne, I need this! Lay down the law. That's what I'll do.

The clock's at 12:34. Not much time, Robert thinks. My back's against the wall. The worst call I've ever had to make. Damn. I've just got to. It's just no good. I can't do this. . . . Can't live with it. Probably go wrong somehow anyway. Dear God, please, I need a lot of help here.

A reporter knocks and comes into Robert's office.

"Tom. No way. Big family problem." Robert waves him back. The same hand keeps going, comes down on the phone, and gets the receiver up to his ear. He winces as he dials. He's shaking from his head to his feet as the number goes through.

Anne's voice, he thinks, let me just hear it.

Busy! Oh, fuck no. I got the courage up, and then it's busy.

Robert waits twenty seconds and pushes the REDIAL button. . . . Busy.

He punches O. "Operator, I need to interrupt a call. A press emergency. Totally urgent. . . . Lady, just make it happen. Life and death. I'm not kidding."

Good, Robert thinks. I'm on a roll now.

He springs up so he can pace by the desk. Listening with angry impatience to the process of breaking into a call. Two minutes go by before the operator comes back and says, "There's no call in progress. Either the phone is off the hook or there's a malfunction. Would you like to report this problem to Service?"

Robert stares at the phone, the operator's words just a grating whirr. Please no, he wants to scream. . . . Don't tell me this. . . . What's it mean? Tell me that! . . . "No," he finally shouts. "I mean yes! You know the damned number. Get it fixed."

He hangs up the phone. His face feels hot and prickly. His body seems to be collapsing, the strength rushing out of him.

Alright, I call the police, send them there for a domestic disturbance. Some bullshit. Anything, just disrupt Kathy's plans. But no, hell, it'd have *criminal* written all over it. How could I make this call? How'd I know enough?

Robert lurches out of his office. Somebody has a cellular phone, who is it? It's lunch. Where is everybody? Why's the phone busy but nobody's on it? He moves to the center of the open area, shouts. "I need a cellular phone. I've got a . . . big story. Now. Now, damn it!"

There's only three people, all staring at him. One of them says, "Here you go. Hey, you people are my witness. The boss has my phone. . . . Whoa . . ."

Robert snatches the phone and starts toward the elevators. He punches in the number, hears the busy signal. He goes down to the street, walking through the soft drizzle toward Grand Central, carrying the phone in his left hand, punching REDIAL every half minute.

What the hell am I doing? . . . I can't stay still. I'm supposed to be over on Sixth a little later for the alibi. Fuck it. Why is the phone off the hook? . . . Maybe it's all over. They had a fight, knocked the phone off. . . . Yeah, but Kathy would put it back, wouldn't she? . . . It's just one of those stupid accidents. That damned cordless phone we've got. The receiver doesn't nestle properly. . . . Hell, we've talked about that. We're both careful. . . . I've just got to start out. I can't stay here.

He reaches Track 23, realizes all his clothes are damp. But not from the light rain.

"Christ," he mutters, pacing six steps one way, then six

steps back, “I’m sweating like a man with malaria or something.”

Anne, he thinks, I really do like you. I love you. You have to understand that. This whole thing just got out of control. Can you forgive me?

He stares down the empty track. I could take a cab, all the way up there. No. The train’s got to be faster.

Maybe it’s all over now.

He pushes the REDIAL button again.

Chapter 36

Kathy follows Anne into the house. Now they're in an open sort of foyer, living room to the left, dining room to the right, steps to the second floor ahead of them. Actually, Kathy thinks, a fairly typical old house, and not very well decorated. I'd make it so much prettier.

"What a lovely home," she says, glancing about, as though admiring the place. Actually making sure the layout she has in her mind is accurate. Feeling pretty good, she thinks, considering. It'll all be over in a few minutes. Easy now. Just do one step at a time. One, two, three.

"Oh, take off that wet coat," Anne says. Watching closely to see whether the woman favors the pocketbook or the coat.

"Oh, alright. . . . Thank you." She puts the pocketbook on the floor by her right foot, as if she doesn't want it to get far away, and takes off the coat.

Anne sees she has a good figure. Damn, she thinks. Never mind. You're not taking anything that's mine.

"Oh, just drape it there." Anne gestures with her right hand at a nearby chair. Doesn't look right, she thinks, I ought to hang it up. . . . It's a good thing people have such lousy manners these days.

"I do hope it's not a bad time," Kathy says casually. "I mean, you don't have friends over or anything, do you?"

Of course, Anne thinks, she's got to be sure I'm alone. It's like a slow pitch over the plate. Well, hit it, girl. "Oh, just Marge . . . unless she's gone." Anne glances uncertainly toward the kitchen.

Kathy stares to her right into the dining room. She can see the door that goes to the kitchen. Is somebody in there? "I'm sorry?" She's smiling brightly as she reaches down and picks up the pocketbook.

"Marge," Anne whispers. "A pest." A thin smile. "So, you might move into our wonderful neighborhood? Phyllis, is it? You want to sit down?"

Kathy isn't liking this. Maybe there's somebody in the kitchen, maybe not. There's definitely something stiff, maybe even tough, about the way the woman's holding herself, the way she's talking. Something not quite right. A pleasant enough woman, just to look at her. Kathy can imagine Robert with her, on his slow days. Still, there may be something wrong. Oh, of course—she is home because she's having a bad period. She could end up in any kind of mood. Maybe that's it.

Right, Kathy thinks, but now what? Ask a few questions and ease on out of here, that might be the best thing. Or switch tactics, just tell her about Robert and me—Hey, lady, give it up. Or I walk over there and look in the kitchen, settle Marge one way or another, and then get on with it? I've still got all my options, I'm in control. One, two, three. . . . "Well," Kathy says calmly, softly, "I really don't want to take that much of your time."

Anne can hardly breathe. Trying to be casual, trying to stay ready. Her left arm is getting stiff from being held in one position. When the woman doesn't want to sit down, Anne becomes even tenser. Oh, it's going to happen *right away?*

"Well, how can I help you?" Anne asks in a tight voice, unable to stop herself from glancing at the pocketbook.

Kathy looks at the other woman, then toward the door into the kitchen. "Really, is there anyone else here? I don't want to intrude."

Anne grins more than she means to. Too much tension. I'm losing it, she thinks.

The two women study each other curiously, as if each can read answers in the other's face.

Kathy knows something is wrong now. She also knows there's no third person in the kitchen. So what the hell is going on? "Look, um, I'll talk to you later. This is probably a bad day." She's still hesitating. "I'll, uh, leave you my card." Trying to keep all her options. Kathy lifts the pocketbook halfway to her chest.

"No," Anne blurts out, her face pale and tense. "You won't do anything. . . . You know why?"

"What?" Kathy pretends not to understand, desperately wanting to know what the woman means. She freezes, the pocketbook motionless in front of her stomach. I could get the knife in a second, she thinks. "What did you say?"

"I, uh, have a recording system in the house. . . . Everything's being recorded." Anne can't stop there. "Sooo—you're the . . . the bitch?"

Kathy's eyes widen. *The bitch?!* Definitely all wrong now. Run? Go for it? Yes, this is a smart woman. Kathy can see that now. But not very happy. In fact, almost rigid with unhappiness. There's not going to be any way to talk to this woman. What now? What do I do? What do I say? How does this woman know who I am? Robie! . . . Kathy can't remember feeling so indecisive.

"I said," Anne says with grotesque emphasis, "so-you-are-the-bitch?"

"I think you are confused—" Kathy sees the tension in the other woman's shoulders and arms, thinks that Anne is about to attack her. Kathy flinches, raises the pocketbook a little more, to protect herself. Anne's left hand jerks up, the elbow still by her ribs, and her fingers snap open less than a foot from Kathy's face. The pepper gets into her eyes and nose. She immediately begins crying and coughing and gagging. "Wait . . . minute," she tries to say, but the words are smothered. She blinks rapidly in an attempt to clear her burning eyes; she can see only light and a few colors. She lets go of the pocketbook. "Help me. . . . " She's backing up, bending over slightly, touching at her eyes with both hands. Thinking, Robie . . . she knew . . . she *knew!* How could you let . . . ?

Anne has already stepped to a nearby table and picked up a Steuben ashtray she put there earlier in the morning. Now she smashes it down as hard as she can on the other woman's forehead, just above the hairline. Kathy's legs give and she kneels on the floor, coughing and stunned. Her eyes clenched shut. She can't move, can't think clearly. Robie—*my Robie*—is vaguely in her consciousness, a small figure getting smaller, and everything she worked for is fading with him.

Anne drops the ashtray and snatches up the pocketbook and rips it open, to find out what kind of weapon is in there.

Chapter 37

Anne stares blankly into the pocketbook. Then she sees the knife in a fold. She lifts it out, stares some more.

"Why, it's . . . *my* knife."

She glances toward the dining room, at the cabinet where the silver is kept. Her heart is beating so wildly, she thinks she might faint. She doesn't hear the other woman's hacking and sobbing. This knife—there's no doubt it's Anne's, a gift that used to belong to her grandmother. There's a fancy script *M*. . . .

Her voice is soft and ghastly. "Oh, Robert. You gave her the knife to . . . Oh, who could think . . . ?"

The knife maddens her. She drops the pocketbook and quickly picks up the ashtray. She hits Kathy again, in the same spot, harder. Again she drops the chunk of glass and pushes Kathy's shoulder so that she sprawls back on the carpet. Anne squats beside her, placing the handle of the knife into Kathy's right palm, careful that the cutting edge is down, the knife the way a person would normally hold it. Kathy is struggling in a weak and disoriented way, maybe not even conscious. She hardly resists.

"You're not taking anything else," Anne tells her.

Anne closes the other woman's gloved hand and forces the hand across so that the blade goes in under Kathy's left breast.

Kathy can't see or understand what is happening. She hardly reacts to the blade sliding into her heart.

Anne pushes down hard on Kathy's fist, moving the knife some. Kathy's body thrashes but without strength. Blood oozes up around the blade. She twitches more feebly.

Anne sees the color vanish out of Kathy's face.

Anne sits back on the rug. Trying to breathe in a normal way. "I thought it might come to this. . . . Maybe I hoped it would. . . ."

She sees for the first time that Kathy's hair is a wig. It's slipped up a few inches. Well, well . . .

Alright, she thinks, work this out. Now or never. . . . The knife, the damned knife . . . should I change the knife? What's the best story? For me . . . for Robert . . . ?

Anne stands up, looks at her clothes, at the room, the carpet. Trying to be sure she catches anything that doesn't fit. She stares down at Kathy.

Anne knows there's something she has to do while she's angry enough to go through with it. She reaches down and seizes Kathy's arms and yanks the woman up, first to her knees, then all the way. Anne shakes her as violently as she can manage, back and forth, and side to side, to mess up her clothes. Then Anne kicks her on both legs and knees her twice. She knows a bite would be a good touch but she can't do it. She lets the body topple backward onto the carpet.

The knife didn't move. Anne kneels down by the dead woman and again folds the limp right hand about the handle of the knife.

Okay, officer, it's like this. The woman came to the door, wanted to ask me some questions about the neighborhood. No, never saw her before. So we're walking and talking, go into the dining room there. And she starts to stare at me, real mean. She opens the cabinet, grabs a knife and comes after me. I grabbed the pepper shaker off the table, opened it and tried to throw pepper at her. We're circling the table and I got some in her eyes. It slowed her down. So I run in here and get this ashtray and, what with the pepper and jumping around, I throw it and hit her pretty good. I was hysterical. We both were. I've probably got this all mixed up. So now we're grappling and I get her hand in mine and I'm kicking and I bent her hand around and stabbed her. And I can tell you, I just hung on until I was sure she wasn't coming after me anymore. Basically, that's it. . . .

Anne holds the woman's hand tight about the handle of the knife for a few more minutes, until she sees it's starting to hold by itself.

"You poor bitch," Anne whispers. "Robert sends you to do what he couldn't. . . . I got that part right. . . . And who are you, Kathy?"

Anne lets go of the knife and walks slowly into the kitchen. She puts the pepper away, cleans up any traces. Then she goes to the dining room table and opens the shaker there, throws some on the table, several places on the floor. She knocks two chairs over. She walks back to Kathy and sprinkles some pepper on her blouse, tosses the shaker across the room. No way she would be accurate in a real fight.

The ashtray? . . . Fine where it is.

Anne stares out the window, sees that a faint rain is still falling. The street gray and empty. Suddenly Anne wonders, Well, how'd she get here?

Anne goes to the coat hanging on the chair, reaches into the pockets. She finds the car keys. She almost drops them. Oh, my God, they're Robert's! . . . He's out there? No, the car's out there. . . . And it couldn't be unless he gave it to her. How can I ever save this man? Never mind whether I should.

Anne makes the decision to keep on trying. She goes to the closet, gets a raincoat. . . . No, she thinks, hanging it up again. She puts on Kathy's coat, uses her umbrella. She leaves the house, walks to the sidewalk, looks both ways. . . . Nothing. Alright, try the nearest corner. As soon as she turns the corner, she sees the car, walks purposefully to it. Glancing nervously about, not seeing anyone. She gets in the car, drives it back to her house, parks it beside her car. Alright, Robie couldn't get it started, he got a cab. . . . No, he got me to take him. Yeah, that's good. I was out this morning. Could have been. . . .

She goes back inside, thinks about what she's done. Terrible thing, she thinks, staring at the dead woman. Well, it's *supposed* to be me there. . . . And then what was going to happen? Robert comes home from a day at the office, finds his dear wife dead, and cries all the way to his next honeymoon.

Anne thinks about Robert. Yeah, he's probably waiting right now for a call. The poor bastard. I'll try to save him. Then I'll never talk to him again.

Not sure she means this, but it sounds right.

Anne wanders into the kitchen, to pull the phone out of the drawer, call the cops. Get on with the second half of her life. No, she thinks. That other Anne's dead. . . . maybe that's not the right way to say that. . . .

She starts to punch 911.

No. . . . She goes down to the basement, unclips the little wires that connect the recorder to the phone lines. Then erases the messages she kept. She thinks about hammering it into little pieces and flushing them down the toilet. Probably hard to do . . . and not necessary.

She remembers a box full of old appliances. She throws the recorder against a cinder block wall two times. Now it looks old and broken. She wipes it clean of prints and puts it in the box with the tape player and the mixer and the slicer. The wires she carefully rolls and puts in the opposite corner of the same box.

Boy, she thinks, you get into this stuff and you can't stop. I'll take it out tomorrow and throw it in the Hudson, if that'll make me feel any better.

Anne walks back to the kitchen, messes her hair, dishevels her clothes, and now she dials 911.

Chapter

38

Robert sees that the train is close to Bronxville. He's staring with crazed eyes at the landmarks that tell him this. Then at his watch. Then at the phone, punching REDIAL again.

Knowing he must look like a mad person. The kind of person they used to put a net over and lock up.

Without any question, he thinks, the worst hour of my life. Each minute of it worse than the one before. There are so many bad possibilities. Something's wrong at the house. There's a dozen things right there. Or everything went right, and I should be in Manhattan now. How can I be an alibi?

But is that what I want?

Robert realizes he can't decide which of the scenarios flashing in his head is the worst. Or if he could choose any one of them, which one he wants. This has to be what hell is, he thinks. Pain like this, you naturally commit suicide after a few hours.

"But in Hell you couldn't. That would be the catch."

Robert realizes he's mumbling out loud. He stares around guiltily, punching REDIAL again.

The phone rings.

Oh, God, he thinks, slumping back heavily in the seat. Is it a trick? Did the number go through right?

Anne answers. "Hello."

He can't speak. He stares at the phone. Then at his watch. It's almost 1:35. Is it a recording?

Suddenly he coughs up some words, "Anne? . . . Robert."

"Hi, Robert. How are you?"

Her voice sounds normal. Completely normal.

"Anne? The phone was busy. . . ."

"That can happen."

"So you're all right?"

"What should be wrong?"

He can't speak. What should he say? He's got to blurt it out. "Anne, there's this woman. . . ."

"Yes?"

"Uhh, she might stop by to talk to you."

Anne chuckles. "What about? More life insurance?"

Robert thinks his heart has stopped. He's wheezing. He can't go on.

"Robert, this call sounds a little funny. Some kind of noise. Where *are* you?"

He can't close his mouth or start talking. He almost screams: *What should I say?*

"Robert, listen. There's not much time. The police are coming over. We had an intruder today."

And what happened? He can't say the words.

"Where are you, Robert? Tell me now."

"Tr-tr-train," he stutters.

"To Bronxville?"

"Yes . . . yes."

"That looks funny, doesn't it? I just called you to tell you what happened, said to come right away. . . . Well, probably you can figure this out."

"You called me?"

"Let's say I did. . . . Oh, I hear them. Robert, one suggestion. Don't say anything before you talk to me."

The phone clicks in his ear. He's stunned. This is worse, this is better? He can't even guess.

But Anne's alive, he thinks. It was her voice. Maybe that's good. Has to be! No murder. There won't be a murder. The cops are coming. There can't be. Great, I hated the thought. There's got to be some other way. . . . But what happened? She said an intruder. Anne didn't say a woman. Maybe some burglar. But look—Anne didn't sound upset. It can't be too bad.

The train is stopping. Robert looks around, realizes he has to stand up, get off the train.

And do what? . . . What was all that, the way she was talking to me? *Doesn't that look bad? You can figure it out.* What's all that?

Robert realizes he can't remember anything clearly. His heart knotted up in his chest, he remembers that. Anne's voice sounded normal. She's alive. These are things he's sure of. But the words . . . What they mean? . . . All of this is drifting away like a shape you think you see in clouds.

That's it—she said to talk to her first. . . . Why'd she say that?

Robert lurches off the train and along the platform. He feels suddenly exhausted, as if he's been awake for twenty-four hours and now he just wants to sleep. He sees it's still raining, but not enough to bother him. He goes down to the parking lot and to his car.

I left it right here, I'm sure. . . .

He stumbles one step backward. . . . Kathy took it!

He puts both hands on his face. It's too much, he thinks. Where is it . . . is she?

He lurches some more, moving back toward the station, to the zone where taxis pull up. He sees one and raises his hand.

Wouldn't that look funny? Anne said that. Cops are there and I come walking in. Does that look funny? . . . Well, why am I fucking there?

Robert shakes his hand at the cabdriver. No . . . no . . . forget it. I'll sit on this bench until I can figure something out. His clothes all feel moldy and heavy. He knows he'll probably get a cold from all the dampness and stress.

Say I just called you, she said. Alright, I go to Grand Central, get the train now. And I'd be here in forty minutes or whatever. Not now. Yeah.

Robert's head feels thin and dizzy. Something is not right . . . but what? Hardly a single word is fixed in his memory. And when he tries to reconstruct what was said, the words fade some more.

More life insurance? Oh-my-God-yes, she said that. Robert coughs and then hits his chest. What a thing. . . . But a serious tone. Like conversation. Had to be an accident. She couldn't make a joke about something like that. . . . I mean, if she knew, well, that was a factor. . . .

Wouldn't that look funny? She said that! I know it. What the hell does that mean? She's standing outside, observing the thing. Saying, Wouldn't that look funny? Funny to who? . . . The police?

Robert leans back, lets his head sag back against the wall. Wouldn't that look funny to the police? . . . She can't say that unless she knows more . . . than she knows.

Something is all wrong. Not something, you idiot. Everything. But something weird. I can't understand this. Oh, Kathy, where are you? There, that car coming into the parking lot. Why can't that be you? You could come waltzing over, explain everything to me. Or you're back in the city already?

No—the car would be here! Where the hell is the damned fucking car? Kathy—did you wreck it? Anne said nothing about a car. Does she know that, too?

I have to wait here. Alright, then I go over to the house.

My wife called, said the police were coming, something about an intruder. She sounded upset so I rushed home. How can I help, officer?

No. . . . Anne said don't talk until we talk. Like I'll fuck it up or something. . . . Fuck *what* up? Yeah, that's definitely the tone. We have to talk, so I won't fuck it up. Thanks, Anne. *We were talking.* Why didn't you just tell me what you have to tell me? I swear to God, I think she . . . meant to leave me hanging. Oh, make me suffer. . . . Come on. That's not Anne.

I'd love to call back . . . get this settled. But she'd just say, Can't talk now. She'd probably be right.

Oh, fuck it. She's alive. That's wonderful. Now if I could see Kathy and the car, everything would be fine. Kathy got far enough to use the car, to be an intruder maybe. Maybe then she failed, and she's upset and just getting drunk. . . . No, maybe this intruder interrupted Kathy's plans, scared her away. Yeah, that makes sense.

What did Anne say right off? What should be wrong? Something like that. Right. Great! *What should be wrong?* That's as good as saying nothing's wrong.

Right. He sighs. Right! Maybe this thing isn't the worst day of my life, after all. The worst hour, for sure. But then the game turns around some. And hell, whatever happened, this forces everything in the open. If Anne knows about Kathy, then we can talk it out. Businesslike. I think the world of Anne. I'm so glad it didn't . . . work out.

Robert shakes his head, then studies his watch. He searches in his pocket for the schedule, so he can know when to arrive. . . . What an idiot. I'll see the next train come in. . . . He tries to laugh. . . . I'll be on it.

•••

The 1:40 roars into the station. Robert is at the end of the platform, so he can mingle with the passengers getting off and walking down to the street.

Alright, he thinks, I'm coming home, just like my wife requested. Hey, all you people, look at me. I just got here.

He finds a cab, gives an address a block away from his house. He wants to approach slowly, see what's going on.

The rain is so slight it's just a mist. The cab's tires make a *wissshhh* sound. Robert feels his body cooling down some. He's more aware of how damp his clothes are. He moves to the left side, so he can see himself in the rearview mirror, see how he looks. Not great, he thinks. He smooths his hair back with both hands. What the hell, I look exactly like a guy who's been running around in the rain. Like almost everybody else. See, something good out of something bad. Maybe we get out of this.

Robert sees two police cars in front of his house, one with a light blinking, two heads in it, facing the other way. Some people standing across the street. What in the hell is going on?

"No, go closer," he tells the driver. Why's he getting off a block away? . . . Might look funny. "Here's okay."

He gets out of the cab and starts toward his house. There's a high shrub to get by and then he sees the ambulance in the drive. Jesus. Somebody's hurt.

He wants to run but thinks he should be casual. He makes a conscious effort to be a tired, overworked guy called home early for no good reason. *The wife, you know.* Otherwise, not a care in this world.

Robert saunters past the cop cars toward the front door. Then he realizes his car is in the drive, too. In front of the ambulance. How the hell did it end up here? he wonders. He sees that the front door is open. A cop is standing just inside the glass storm door, with his back turned to Robert.

Robert knocks and opens the glass door. "Hi," he tells the startled cop, "I'm Mr. Saunders. I live here."

"Yeah. Come on in." The cop smiles. "Your wife's a little upset."

Robert starts to say, "Well, what happened?" Then he remembers what Anne said. Talk to me first. Okay, *okay*.

Robert shrugs as if he expected this, as if he expected all of this. "Right," he says. "That's understandable. Where is she?"

"Kitchen, I think. They're talking back there." The cop points out the way to his own kitchen.

Stupid cop, Robert thinks as he steps past the blue uniform into the foyer. He sees two medics in the living room, standing and chatting. He glances down at the white mound on the floor. What?! It's just like on TV or something, got to be a body, who the hell . . . ? And this glimmer goes through his brain. It's all he can do not to shout out the question, *Who* is *that?"* Or run over and pull back the sheet. His body temperature seems to drop ten degrees. He gasps and tries to cover this by coughing. Then he thinks, No, no way, just stay calm. *What could be wrong?* That's what she said. . . .

As he walks rightward into the dining room he makes himself look again. It is a woman, almost definitely. . . . The intruder? Anne said intruder. Anne killed an intruder? How the hell could that be? Somebody killed an intruder? Damn, they don't cover the face unless somebody's dead. . . .

Robert hears the voices now. Men and women, sounds like. He reaches the door to the kitchen, sees three people, Anne, a man at the table with her, and a female cop standing back.

They all look at Robert as he comes through the door. "Oh, Robert," Anne says, "I'm glad you're here. Detective Gillson, this is my husband, Robert. He came up from Manhattan." The men nod, then shake hands, say hello.

Robert notices the little tape recorder on the table.

Anne goes on: "Could I possibly take a break? I feel lousy in every possible way." She comes around the table, not waiting for an answer, and rushes to Robert and hugs him, pressing her face on his chest. "It's been awful," she mumbles.

Robert holds her, says, "It's all right, Anne. Don't worry."

Wondering if that makes any sense. Thinking that he has her in his arms, the woman he thought he would never see alive again. Great, wonderful. Anne's still here. But who's that in the living room? It can't be. . . .

Anne raises her head, stares into his eyes. A strange, flat look. As if she's not sure she knows him, or she's waiting for something. . . .

Robert glances past her, sees the detective watching him. He feels he has to say something. "This is rough," he tells the cop. "Can she take a break? Can I walk her around some?"

The detective's a thin, somehow lazy-looking man. He shrugs as if everything's okay with him. *The good cop*, Robert thinks, writing the story in his head.

Anne squeezes his arm. "Yes," she sighs, "walk me around. I've got a lot of aches," she says as if PMS is really her main problem.

They go through the dining room toward the living room. Now they're walking along arm in arm, the white mound ten feet ahead. Robert stares at it and again chills go through his body. Anne doesn't seem to notice it. The medics see them coming. One says, "Ask Gillson when he thinks we can leave."

Anne leads Robert past the body, into the rear of the living room. Three windows look out at the backyard. A grand piano is there, and Anne and Robert stand behind the bench, staring out at the wet lawn.

"Hold me, Robert." She snuggles in close to him, tilting her face on his chest. "Listen closely, my dear. Do not say or do anything. Got that?"

"Yes." Not liking her tone very much.

"My guess is that they'll figure out you know her. I suggest you admit it but play it down to half or a quarter of what it was. Unless you think you can deny ever knowing her. . . . Would you be able to pull that off?"

Her? "Her? Her who?"

"I'm trying to save you, Robert. You're guilty of accessory to attempted murder. Please listen."

"Accessory to what?" Robert turns slightly so he can see her face better. She seems so composed. Sort of brittle, perhaps, but not emotional. What is she saying? I *know* her? Even if I do, how does Anne know? Who is it anyway? Murder? She's way ahead of me or way behind, I can't figure it. . . .

"Please, Robert. I'm doing the best I can. That woman, Kathy—"

"Kathy?!"

Anne sees the strange pinched look in his face. He hasn't gotten it yet. "Robert-do-not-move-or-raise-your-voice. Yes, that's Kathy." She feels his body twitch. "But it's important you didn't know she was going to do this. She did it on her own."

All Robert can think is: That's not Kathy. It's impossible. Somehow there's a mix-up here. Anne kill Kathy? There's no way.

"Robert, please concentrate. Rub my back. About the car . . . I brought it back. You couldn't get it started. I took you to the train this morning. All right?"

"Right, right. Why do you keep saying . . . her name is Kathy?"

"About the knife—"

Robert gasps, "The knife?"

"Forget about it entirely. She found it here."

Robert looks stricken now. His mouth hangs open, unable to make more words. The knife . . . the knife . . . Anne knows about a knife. Kathy had a knife. . . . What does it mean?

"Now I suggest you don't talk to them until you have a lawyer. Stall a day or two. Get your thoughts together. But I think it might be appropriate if you went over and asked to look at the body. Then you're completely amazed that it's her. And, of course, shocked. Just say 'Oh, my God' a lot."

Robert is staring at her. He seems to be catatonic. Anne

has a sad feeling that all this effort might be wasted. She'll try to save Robert and he'll drag them both down. Well, I'll tell the truth—I lied to save my poor love-befuddled husband. What else should a wife do?

Anne hears people moving near the front door.

"Robert, am I getting through at all? They might be about to carry her away. . . . Kathy. Go ahead. See for yourself."

Robert stares at her some more, his eyes blinking. He pulls away from her, turns toward the body, almost stumbling. "I can't believe this," he says over and over as he moves toward the sheet. A cop and two medics are looking at him now. He's thinking about everything Anne said, and how if she's right, then this is Kathy. And if it is, then he should be surprised she's here. Anne's right. . . . He glances for a second back at her. "I can't believe this. None of it." He lurches closer, until his shoes almost touch the hem of the sheet. He looks at the form, then at the faces watching him. He sees Gillson coming in from the dining room.

Robert starts breathing deeply, his eyes getting wilder, not acting, just not hiding what he was feeling all along. "My wife thinks I might know this person. I've got to look. I have to. Is it okay?"

The medics look at Gillson and he shrugs and says, "Said her name was Phyllis Bender. You know her?"

"No." Robert's face fills with gratitude for a few seconds. See, a mix-up.

"But the wallet says Kathy Becker."

"Oh, no! This is horrible. . . ."

"Yeah, we need an ID—"

Robert squats down and pulls the sheet up a few inches. For an instant he thinks it might still be someone else. There are two moles or something. The face is so pale except under the eyes. The eyelids are red and clenched shut. She's been crying, he thinks. He lifts the sheet a little more, so he can clearly see her mouth, her chin, the rise of her breasts. . . . The blood there. . . . Oh, yes, it is. It is. . . .

The two words repeat themselves, like some odd prayer for her, for the rest of his life when he won't ever see Kathy alive. It is. It is all over. It is her. It is . . . beyond reason. There's no way this can be Kathy. So strong, so full of life, so clever and resourceful and brave.

He feels the eyes on him and looks up. "I do know her. . . . She works at the paper in the city." Then he thinks about what Anne said and he adds, "I had no idea. . . . You can't believe what a shock this is. . . . She was a . . . good friend."

The medics exchange glances at that. Even Gillson shrugs and looks away. Yeah, buddy, *good friend.*

Robert wishes he could pull the sheet off and lie down beside her, press himself against her one last time, kiss her cold skin. Kathy, wake up. I loved you, I truly did. I do. . . .

He stands up slowly. "I can't get over this. It's madness."

He turns some and sees Anne still standing near the piano. Watching him with the same flat expression. "I'm sorry, Anne. . . . I did know her. But you have to believe me, I never thought . . ." He trails off.

"Thought what?" Gillson butts in.

Robert looks at him in amazement. Are you an idiot? "Thought she'd come up here . . . and did . . . whatever she did. . . . I don't understand it yet."

"You ready to talk to me?" Gillson says. "Read him his rights," the detective says to the cop by the door.

"Sure, do that," Robert says vaguely. "But no, I can't talk now, if you don't mind. I'm going to be numb for a while."

He drifts back to Anne. She takes his arm and they stand facing the cops and medics.

"Okay, boys, move out," Gillson tells his people. The medics go to lift Kathy's stretcher. "We'll pick it up later, Mr. and Mrs. Saunders. I'm not sure what we got here. Probably just straight self-defense. Never mind. We have to go through the process. Just be patient. I'm sorry, Mrs. Saunders, you have to come along now. Talk today, Mr. Saunders? Tomorrow?"

Anne says, "Whatever you say. Give me a few more minutes."

"Whatever," Robert says vaguely. "How about first thing in the morning?"

"Fine, fine," Gillson says, turning to go out the door.

They watch the last cop file out of their home. Robert wants to ask what really happened. "Anne, please . . ." he says quietly. "I'm lost. Can you tell me what . . . went on here?"

"The detective has a very full statement, Robert. You could read that when you're ready. Basically, I confessed."

Robert stares at her, confused by her strange detachment. "Confessed . . . ?"

"You probably ought to see your lawyer now," she says, "get ready for tomorrow. I'll be all right at the station. I'm not sure about bail. Robert, call Gillson in an hour or two." She smiles briefly. "I don't want to spend the night in a jail."

"No, of course not."

He watches her intently. There, they're planning together, working things out.

"And, Robert . . . I don't want you to stay here tonight."

Robert forgets his questions. He stares in surprise. "Anne . . . please. Like you said, I had no idea . . . it would come to this."

Anne laughs in a dry, sorrowful way. "I suppose not. Anyway, part of the deal is that you leave. Our lawyers will work out the details. I expect you not to quibble."

"Anne. What are you saying? . . . I love you, Anne. No matter what you think, I do." He confronts her. "Don't you love me?"

"I do, Robert. Probably I always will. But I cannot live with you." Her face is cold and sad. "You have to leave."

"Anne, this isn't . . ."

"Think what you did, Robert. . . ."

Robert thinks his head will vibrate into pieces. "Please, Anne. I need you. I'm just so sorry. . . . I need a second chance."

"Haven't you been paying attention at all? I just gave you one."

Robert settles down on the nearest chair. Head in his hands. He thinks he'll cry. Then he realizes there's nothing left.

Anne realizes she feels sorry for him. She almost reaches out to touch his hair but stops herself. She thought she was going to be enraged, screaming at Robert, insulting him. Now she actually feels sorry for him. What a thing. And that woman in the ambulance. Yes, sorry for her, too.

But, Anne thinks, not so sorry I'd take it all back. I'm supposed to be dead now, I should be happy. I wish I felt something. And here I am, a little sorry, nothing else. Sorry for Robert and me and that woman.

"Please, Anne, think about it," Robert suddenly says.

Anne sighs. "I can't imagine not thinking about it."

He looks away from her intent face, toward the rug where Kathy was lying under the sheet. "You actually killed her?" he asks.

"Yes."

"Just you?"

"Yes!"

Robert stares at her again. There's something stern in her face. He doesn't remember seeing this before.

"How could you do it?"

"The truth? I guess I didn't like the idea of being pushed around."

His eyes widen. "I didn't mean . . . why. Oh, God, pushed around? . . . I mean how."

Anne shrugs. "My lucky day, I guess."

Robert cannot bear the blank look in her face, the flat tone of her voice. "And you want me to leave?"

"Yes."

Something cold and implacable. My sweet wife Anne. . . .

"Anne, please. . . . Lucky day? No, it's horrible. It's not real. It's too much to deal with. Alright, I'll go. And we'll talk . . . again."

"I'm sure we will. Well, Robert, I have to go now. I'm being booked, I think it is. This will be in the papers, you know. . . . You might want to think about that when you talk to your lawyer."

"Meaning . . . what?"

"Making sure your story sounds right, Robert. You know how they bore away at these things."

Robert just stares at her. In the papers? She means us, me. . . . Robert sees his name in a headline . . . their photos . . . Kathy's pretty face. He lurches to his feet. "*How*, Anne? How in God's name? . . . You actually killed her?"

Anne walks to the foyer to get her coat.

Chapter 39

Stan touches his fingers, stares across his desk at Anne. His face twitching now and then. "Are you really sure you want me to handle this? I mean, I just don't know. . . ."

Anne smiles faintly, sitting back in the big stuffed chair. It amuses her that Stan's so nervous. "I've told you once, Stan. That should be sufficient. I thought you liked this kind of case."

"What kind?"

"Somebody breaks in somebody's house."

"I believe you let her in."

"Of course. Well, then. Somebody comes into somebody else's house in order to commit a crime. Or you only like to represent the bad guy?"

Stan fidgets some more. "No, not at all. It's just that . . ."

"Stan, really, what is the problem? You think I'm the bad guy?"

"Anne . . . this is a very serious matter. What do you find so amusing about it?"

Anne figures it's really because of Stan and the other lawyers, telling those stories in the cafeteria, that Kathy's dead now. It's his baby. And she thinks he should have it to the end.

"I don't think I can tell you that. I'm sorry, Stan. I'll try to be more serious. So what's the gossip around here?" She pauses before asking: "Will I . . . *do time?*"

"Now, there," Stan snaps at her. "Don't talk like that. It doesn't sound as if you care."

"I'm all out of caring about very much, Stan." She shrugs, sitting there in her dark suit, her hair combed back more than it used to be, looking quite sophisticated. "Anyway, I want you on the case. I want you to do a first-rate job. The police have a statement on tape and another on video. I co-operated fully. Contact Gillson and get copies."

"You didn't have a lawyer present," Stan says. "That testimony could all be challenged."

"No, we won't be doing any challenging around here. But I'll say this. The whole thing was fast, violent, and terrifying. I can't vouch for the exact sequence of events. I expect your only job will be to keep them from building a case based on small discrepancies. I was home, as you know, because I was sick."

Stan keeps staring at her, a nervous disbelief on his face. He thought she didn't like him. He also thought she was much more high strung than she seems to be now—after something that should make anyone high strung. He certainly never imagined she could kill anyone. The whole thing feels odd. There might be layers he doesn't know about. He's heard, oh, about six theories already on what *really* happened.

"What is it, Stan? Office gossip getting to you? Afraid of getting your name in the papers?"

"None of that bothers you?"

Curious, she thinks. No, it doesn't. I don't seem to care so much what other people think. Now I understand Edd better. People assume he's boring or there's not much to him. He simply doesn't care enough to try to impress anyone.

"Oh," she says. "I was thinking about your question. No, not that much, Stan. Of course, that doesn't mean you can be part of the gossip. You're on my side now."

"Very well, Anne, if you're sure you want me to represent you."

"Very sure, Stan. It just feels right."

Stan shakes his head, not at all comfortable with anything mystical, psychic, or astrological. He's starting to suspect that Anne is operating in there somewhere.

Anne stands to leave. "Call me when you need me, Stan."

Stan stands, too, and reaches over to shake her hand. "Very well, Anne."

"By the way, Stan. I passed Estelle in the hall. I happened to mention a certain promotion I might be willing to litigate over. Of course, I'd want you to handle that."

"Anne! Sue my own firm?"

"Oh, I don't think it'll come to that. . . . I sense she's looking at me in a new way now."

Stan sits down, his face aghast.

Anne winks at him, and then walks into the hall and back toward the elevator to return to her floor. People look up when she passes. There she goes, a bona fide killer. Is that the saddest thing in the world, Anne wonders, or the funniest? She can't decide.

She stops by Edd's office, sits on the corner of his desk. "Well, Edd, how's tricks?"

He leans back, smiling at her. "You're handling all this very well."

"The worst is over. I think anyway. Well, Edd, does this mean I should learn to play bridge?"

"Absolutely not. Bridge ruins a lot of marriages, you know. When you say *this* . . . ?"

"Oh, you remember. You said if you could ever be of help."

"Just name it."

"We'll have dinner, I suppose."

They stare at each other for a long time in silence. Anne thinking about that little favor he did for her, getting that case dropped. Very touching, she always thought that. But she couldn't let herself be touched then. Now she can.

Chapter

40

Tuesday, after a three-drink lunch, Robert goes out to Newark for the funeral. He wears dark glasses, the ones Kathy gave him, and tries not to look at anyone. He keeps his head down, hoping he'll be lost in the crowd. More than two hundred people show up; only a few knew her, the rest read her story in the papers and want to see the end of it. Robert is sweaty and nervous. He can't glance at the coffin without seeing Kathy naked, crawling over the bed toward him, her breasts swinging, grinning at him in that way of hers, doing something he never thought of before. That or he starts blaming himself again, knowing he put her in the ground.

He can finally think it. *Yes, I did it. I killed her. . . .*

But two people come up and say almost the same thing, "We understand, man, it wasn't really your fault. She went too far."

They look at him as if he's a hero for having this flashy

girlfriend. How could he know she'd get nuts and go running up to Westchester to kill his wife? The crazy broad. Show some class.

He's afraid to acknowledge this attitude or say anything for fear it'll vanish. He just nods grimly.

The same slant is in a lot of the coverage. He thought everyone would be against him. It's only four days since it happened, but people are mostly sympathetic. Some of the ones at work sort of joking with him: *Now* we know why you were so crazy. . . . Hardly anyone thinks he's part of it, because then there would have been two against the wife, and she wouldn't have made it. But the crazy girlfriend, by herself, hell, she's bound to make a mess of it.

At the end of the service a woman comes up to him. "We have a lot in common," she says.

"Really? What?"

"She was my best friend. Yours, too, I gather. My name's Louise."

"Your best friend? She never said much about her friends."

"Yeahhhh," Louise says. "She was ready to move on." The woman looks at him with a crooked grin. Squaring her shoulders some, making him notice her build. He looks at it, then shakes his head. Jesus, Robert thinks, it's weird. Like we're supposed to jump on the ground and screw in memory of Kathy.

"Listen," Robert says nervously, "that guy there with the police? At least I think they're police." Robert points to the edge of the crowd, a tough-looking black-haired man standing between two men in gray suits. "He keeps looking at me. You know him?"

Louise snickers. "That'd be Keith."

"Keith?"

"Her ex, you know."

"Really?"

"Didn't mention Keith either, did she?"

"No, she didn't. Not by name."

"She was ready to move on, like I said. You were her ticket. Seriously." She leans closer, grinning, letting him smell her perfume, maybe look down between her breasts. "How'd you make such a mess of it?"

Robert stares at her with a horror he can't conceal. He can't get out a word, finally turns and jogs away from her. Louise looks after him with a certain disgust on her face.

Chapter

41

Robert's lawyer goes out of the room to find some papers. Anne and Robert are in big leather chairs a few feet apart. Robert whispers loudly at her, "Anne, don't you see, it was all a mirage. It wasn't real. None of it. I love you. Please. We shouldn't be divorced. What if we just had a trial separation?"

"No. I can't live with you."

He hates the cool way she's watching him. "It was like a disease. A fever." Robert leans closer to her, his face animated and intense. "The fever's over now. I'm myself again."

Anne ignores what he said. "You know, Robert, you shouldn't have started the affair. But you did. So you had to be able to finish it. Seems to me—and I'm putting this the way I think she would—you screwed up coming and going. Have I got this right?"

Robert stares at her in shock. She's so cold. "That's looking back at it," he insists. "I'm telling you the whole thing was like a hallucination."

"So which are you most sorry about?" Anne says. "I think I can handle this now."

"What?"

"That you started or that you couldn't finish? Which do you regret the most? Tell me!"

"Anne, stop this. That's all hindsight. It was madness, pure and simple."

"Robert—tell me what you're most sorry about. You started the whole thing? Or you couldn't finish it off?" She smiles at him and whispers, "Finish me off, that is."

I can't believe this, Robert thinks. We're married all these years and now she's looking at me with this supercilious expression. I've created a monster. Doesn't she understand? I've lost the most here . . . the two best women I've had in my life.

"Anne, what's happened to you?"

"I survived. What's happened to you, Robert?"

Look, he thinks, she's toying with me. This is horrible. "Anne, please . . . can't you forgive me?"

"No, Robert. I cannot. . . . Don't feel too bad, I'm not sure I can forgive me either."

"Why, Anne? Why?! Why's it have to be . . . like this?"

He's very near her now. She stares quietly into his frantic eyes, studies the big face. Maybe for the last time, she thinks. Look, Robert, it's like this. I defended myself and my home—well, that's part of what happened.

She frowns for an instant, thinking through to the end of it. And I guess I defended myself from the thought, every day for the rest of my life, that you'd be making love to another woman. . . . One you loved more than me. . . .

He blinks before her calm gaze. "I couldn't help myself, Anne. Don't you understand that? I was powerless. I'm only human."

Robert springs from the chair and paces the side of the

room. Looking back at her with imploring grimaces. She watches his big, restless figure.

"Make some allowance," he tells her.

That was the oddest part, she thinks. All the time he was with that other woman, preparing to kill me, really, the marriage was very good. Sex was getting better all the time. It's so weird.

Robert points at her. "I don't accept this, Anne. One mistake? That's all I ever made." He's shouting now. "Do I have to pay for it forever?"

"I guess we all do."

"I want you to be my wife. We belong together."

Anne wonders if she could want Robert back. Is she taking some sick pleasure in rejecting him? Maybe. Probably. How could anyone be sure? It's not just that she can't forgive him or can't understand him; maybe she could do both. But there's the feeling that she has grown in some other direction, where he can't follow her. And she wants to make this definite.

"Tell me this, Robert."

"What? What! Anything!"

"How was the sex?"

"What?!"

"The sex, Robert—with Kathy?"

"Anne! Don't talk like that—"

Robert's lawyer comes back, almost running into the room. "Hey, hold it down. People are listening to—"

"Anne! . . . God, please stop that. What a terrible thing to say."

The lawyer holds Robert's elbow. "Come on, take it easy. These things are always rough."

"Anne, please . . . forgive me." He's trying to push past the lawyer.

She stares across the room, hardly hearing him now.

• Bruce Deitrick Price grew up in Virginia Beach, Virginia, and decided at age seventeen to become a novelist. He graduated from Princeton, served two years in the army, and then settled in New York to pursue a career as a writer. He published a nonfiction book about explorers, and then his first novel, *Ralph*. He worked at a variety of part-time jobs before he started his own business, Word-Wise Advertising, which designs brochures and logos. His second novel, *American Dreams*, was published in 1984. In addition to fiction, he writes poetry and essays on language and eduction. He is also a painter who has had several shows.

Printed in the United States
By Bookmasters